JACOB'S LADDER

About the Author

John A. Williams reported from Africa for *Newsweek* in 1964 and 1965 where, in Lagos, Nigeria, he interviewed Malcolm X. Williams also worked for National Educational Television (NET) in Nigeria. He has since made two tours on the continent. Now the author of eleven novels, seven non-fiction books and editor or co-editor of six other works, Williams currently is Professor of English and Journalism at Rutgers University.

Other Books by John A. Williams

The Berhama Account

!Click Song

The Junior Bachelor Society

Mothersill and the Foxes

Captain Blackman

The King God Didn't Save

The Most Native of Sons

Sons of Darkness, Sons of Light

The Man Who Cried I Am

This Is My Country Too

Sissie

Africa: Her History, Lands and People

Night Song

One for New York

JACOB'S LADDER

a novel by
John A. Williams

THUNDER'S
MOUTH
PRESS
NEW YORK

Copyright © 1987 by John A. Williams

All rights reserved

Published in the United States by

THUNDER'S MOUTH PRESS,

54 Greene Street, 4S, New York, NY 10013

Design by Loretta Li

Grateful acknowledgement is made to the

New York State Council on the Arts and

the National Endowment for the Arts

for financial assistance with

the publication of this work.

Portions of this book were previously

published by River Styx and Essence.

Library of Congress Cataloging-in-Publication Data

Williams, John Alfred, 1925–

Jacob's ladder.

I. Title.

PS3573.I445J3   1987   813'.54   87-1881

ISBN 0-938410-41-5

ISBN 0-938410-76-8 (pbk.)

Distributed by Consortium Book Sales

213 E 4th Street. St. Paul, MN 55101

612-221-9035

Manufactured in the United States of America

In order to emerge or simply survive as a race,
we thought that the only alternative was to steal
the conqueror's weapons, which, incidentally,
they were offering to us, secure in the knowledge
that they would not be turned against them.

LÉOPOLD SÉDAR SENGHOR

JACOB'S LADDER

P R O L O G U E

Out beyond, the ocean heaved in a deep, unhurried rhythm, unleashing waves in long, powerful, frothing blue-green assaults upon the beach except where it struggled through a neck, suffering a constriction; there the water boiled and roared in a hissing fury. But, spraying through, the sea of flying torrent and speeding mist collapsed within the inlet, subsided into restless waves, then wavelets, and flowed serenely, almost reverently, into the perfectly round body of water that was overhung by the great trees of the rain forest. Between the sound of the waves there was a silence in which there seemed to be another, different, sound.

And now it begins.
There are always beginnings.
So close to our place.
Just where it ought to be.

He brought his gaze in from the sea, from that barely visible white sand beach where great cobras used to lay slack in the rising and dying sunlight. His gaze drifted inward from the beach, from the neck, from the sighing waters of the inlet, past the gray buildings that were emitting wisps of smoke. Scabs on a wound already festering, he thought, a wound alien to the place; a wound that had already been embraced by membranes: vines, whose leaves had browned quickly. In this place. Here deaths were mourned and ancient absences grieved, it seemed, by the forests that hugged the edges of the inlet like great dark sentinels.

It will make sun that will not remain fixed.
That sun will be Terror, as when the earth rolls over.
There was no other way.
No. History is a road whose direction is easily seen.

From here, he thought, right from here, they left in their hundreds of thousands. The legends whined and darted at him like insects. But once, it was still sung on the *kora*, the remnants of the Tribes, flushed with anger, their hatred and their desperation, gathered in great longboats, armed with old muskets, clubs, spears, bows and arrows. They blocked the neck, trapping the ships inside the inlet. The ships, echoing the lamentations of the Tribes chained within, could not get wind for their sails. The attack had been planned between the ebb and flow of the tides, the falling and rising of the winds. All their cannons and muskets and swords could not help the Oyinbo. The decks of the ships were scoured with their blood. Those Tribes were freed and the ships were burned and sunk across the neck.

4

But more Oyinbo returned in more ships and with more cannons and more muskets, and they cleared the neck and for nearly half a thousand years emptied the continent of its Tribes. The rain forest remembered, he liked to think, even if some men forgot—or worse—no longer cared. Jija was a sacred place. The closest village was ten miles away. Underfoot here at Jija Deep (for that's what it was called to distinguish it from Jija Near, the village that was ten miles away) lay links from chains, rusted red like the earth in which they rested; and the aged stone foundations of the barracoons stuck out whitely like pieces of bone of an unearthed skeleton.

He looked around. This forest with its great trees of iron and ebonywood, its palms, was bright with flowers: violets of a deeper blue, a sadder blue than anywhere else on the globe, thumbergias, moonflowers, bougainvillea, flamboyant. A petal—blue, pink, red, yellow—for each soul that had vanished beyond the sea; here their spirits still lived and were as multitudinous as the leaves on the trees that tried to conceal them, as many as the daggles of sunlight that pierced the forest and sparkled like diamonds on its floor.

He did not turn at the sound of the footfall; it could be no one but Shaguri. Shaguri said nothing when he came up, a heavy French cologne drifting about him. The two men smiled at each other. The smiles formed slowly, the way lava takes form. Wordlessly they turned to go back down the path to the tree-covered road that led to concealed places staffed by men and machines, and also to cleared, flat places, like farm fields that had been deserted.

"Sssss!" Shaguri stopped suddenly and leaned his body in the way, blocking the path. He looked at Shaguri, followed his glance. There in a still green haemanthus sapling, coiling so slowly that it seemed a part of the bush moving in an unfelt breeze, was a green viper. They backed carefully out of range. Shaguri said, "Pray, Fasseke, we find no vipers slithering in our new bush."

Out of range of the serpent, they proceeded to the road, peering intently at every bush and limb that dangled across their passage. Like other animals, serpents had families. Once he turned back and glanced at the sky above the ridge from which they'd just descended; the lean streams of faint smoke were still rising.

In the helicopter, exactly one fourth of Shaguri's fleet of these craft, they circled once around the buildings and then, nose tilting slightly downward, rushed over the green and brown landscape, over the area where Pandemi, Temian, and Ulcuma (with its bothersome border claims), merged, forests melting into forests, southward to his waiting car.

O N E

Beneath a cloudless sky, a swollen red sun lowered itself down the west into the gently moving blue and purple sea. The sun diffused its burnished red and orange corona far out across the sky with a glow so brilliant that it seemed to continue on forever.

Over the land, birds of all sizes and colors appeared to hang motionlessly in a sudden, windless, color-fractured sky; beasts, large and small, sensing or feeling the sun going down, crept out of the forests, savannahs, and mountains to feed. People paused without knowing they did or why.

When the top of the sun sank beneath the sea, for the length of time it takes to blink an eye, the universe was suddenly illuminated by the blinding silver-green light that raced in pursuit of the fading red and orange glow, flared mightily, and then winked out. No imagined sound could have accompanied the spectacle. It always happened in silence. The Green Flash was gone.

Chuma Fasseke had seen this Green Flash—had happened to look up from his desk toward the west—from his office on the third floor of the Pandemi Government Building. Sometimes, even when you watched for it, you never saw it.

And now the wind came streaking in off the ocean. Rushing inland, it raged through the fringed leaves of the banana trees, and the sound was like a sudden downpour of rain; the wind caused the palm leaves to clatter like irreverent ghostly applause.

Fasseke inhaled deeply and turned his chair to intercept the full force of the wind whipping through his screened open windows. The wind stroked his body. He felt it wriggling desperately through the hair on his head. Fasseke heard it beating through the screens and louvered windows of other offices of the building, and he imagined it scurrying through the halls and dancing with loose papers. The coming of the evening wind always raised Fasseke's spirits, armed him to finish the rest of the day's work, though the days now seemed to have no end and no beginning; just punctuation they were, like the coming of the wind.

However, there were always moments during the day, before the wind came, when Fasseke thought of England and the United States, where coolness was measured not in hours, but in months. He considered those places with mixed feelings: fondness, especially for America, because there were so many folk there who resembled him and were, in fact, related to him by color and history. There was less of that in England. Dislike verging on hatred because those

8

were the places where the enemy resided, wholly uncon-
scious that they were enemies.

Yet, emerging from the Pandemi bush so many years ago to
immerse himself in "education and culture" had been the
precise kind of shock then needed to start him along the road
that led to this office.

His stay in England and the United States had confirmed
in almost equal degree his impressions of peoples who did
not understand the world but liked it just the way it was.
There was a thing so deeply planted in those nations that it
could never be weeded out; a thing so completely taught and
so perfectly absorbed on a less than conscious level that
Fasseke knew centuries would come and go before that thing
was destroyed.

Fasseke heard the Pan Am flight taking off to the east,
sundering the darkening sky. He recalled the long flight out
of New York; it left at seven in the evening, pounding in a
slow curve above Manhattan into the already black heavens.
The plane arrived at Dakar with the morning tide and the
rising sun; Dakar, Bagui, Lagos, and on across the continent
to Nairobi. The jet was now crackling and booming like
thunder fading away.

The takeoffs and landings no longer reminded him that
Pandemi had no national airline. Once it had disturbed him
that Pandemi had no rakish European structures looming in
the center of the business district, little of the glitter and
splash that seemed to smack of the second half of the twen-
tieth century. Fasseke had held to his vision. "These things,"
Shaguri had said, Shaguri, whose country did have an airline
and many glass-fronted high buildings in the capital of his

country, and wide paved roads that ended abruptly and narrowly in the red dirt a few feet from the center of the capital, "These things," he had said, "would seem to be a matter of prestige for us." He had winked. "Even if Temian is drowning in oil, they would want us to behave as they think Africans behave, Fasseke, wouldn't you think?" He'd considered his remark and then amended it. "*Especially* if we have oil."

Fasseke sat back and watched, contented then to lease landing rights and to register foreign ships cheaply under the Pandemi flag. (Pandemi itself had but two freighters, both of which sailed on borrowed time.) Not yet a decade into independence, Fasseke had thought, and the others had run off to the Dutch for Fokkers, to the British for Comets or VC-10s, to the French for Caravelles, and to the Americans for 707s. They had gone not only for the planes, but for all the gadgetry of the other world that presented the veneer of colonialism. They had merely gone from one form of colonialism to another. Independence was a western word, and it was usually garnished in Africa with celebration, spectacle, and high-flown speeches, and with promises flung like sucked fishbones to the wind. It was all more like a disease than the wind O'Brien said was sweeping the continent.

For Patrice independence had meant death, as it had for Hammerskjold; for want of it Chief Luthuli and Nelson Mandela remained trapped in that vast concentration camp to the south; for others there had been shattering, fiery deaths, disappearances; for Roberto independence meant duplicitous strivings; for Jomo, a chance to invite more British back to Kenya than had been there before the "emergency." Wherever one looked, independence had not truly come. And hadn't that British fool in Rhodesia just recently declared "unilateral independence"?

There was, still, in every part of Africa, struggle. For there were many Europeans who were unwilling to grant this grand, empty thing, who refused to partake of ceremony, would celebrate no fraud, and who would never offer membership to Africans in commonwealths or families of nations. The struggle went on even as the bushbeaters of foreign companies slipped across the continent like vipers, stalking oil, uranium, cobalt, ferrochrome, bauxite, gold, iron, copper, diamonds. They trapped and manipulated the crops of groundnuts, cocoa, palm oil, bananas, coffee, tea, and rice. And they still needed the rubber, Fasseke told himself. The rubber, don't forget the rubber.

He had decided, long before he took office six years before, amid the dust left swimming in the air by the Franklins' hasty departure, that things would change in Pandemi if nowhere else in Africa. Yes, people suffered. But they'd always suffered with no end of it to be sighted. There had been none of the miracles the African spirit demands. Wages had creaked upward slowly. New schools, to be placed strategically around the country to satisfy all the groups, were still on the drawing board; new black-topped roads, running not just through the center of Bagui, but through all the towns to the most distant villages, lengthened slowly. It took almost as much time to transport crops from the south by truck as it did when he was a boy. Today, Fasseke thought, today will mark the evidence of change. Six long years coming.

Now he got up and walked to the windows that overlooked the city. He felt a luxurious exhaustion that made him recall the smiling Kru fishermen sailing their boats through the last breakers before gliding in to beach them, their nets already drying in the rigging, their decks silver with fish.

However it was measured, the day had been one of the longest since he'd held the office. Not even Yema knew how long it had been.

Through the window he could see people starting to leave the building. Jeeps filled with soldiers prowled the grounds. The guard was doubled at dusk these days. Traffic was starting to build in Franklin Boulevard. Even he thought of it with the old name though he himself had renamed it—The Avenue of Africa. Baguians who'd never been to Europe or America or to Dakar or Lagos thought the traffic horrendous. Fasseke smiled and prayed that neither Bagui nor any other city in Pandemi would become like those places. In the cars down there, the British hand-me-downs from Sierra Leone, the French-used Deux and Trois Cheveaux, the Renaults, the Volkswagens, the Fiats, rode Pandemi's middle class. They were going to homes built by the Italian architects the Franklins had brought in. They were a few doctors and lawyers, managers of businesses owned by Europeans and Americans, Lebanese merchants, and workers of varying ranks at the several embassies in Bagui.

They lived in the Ashmun and Greenville sections of the city and they hated him. They wished for the return of the Franklins or people like them. The middle class longed for the high old times the Franklins had provided—dances, dinner parties, rallies. The homes to which they were now driving, to be waited upon by their "boys" and "girls," those Italian structures, were now anachronisms that he, Fasseke, allowed to exist. A middle class was the cement, the mortar between those below and those above. It created the illusion, sometimes the fact, that it was possible to swim upward away from one's historical destiny, through one age into another, as it had happened in his own family. Franco had created a middle class and it was still growing; had grown in fact faster than any other in Europe. And Americans boasted of their middle class. The Franklins' middle class had been too small and too greedy.

The rain forests pressed in upon Pandemi's middle class in Bagui, pushed in from the east; the sea shouldered in from the west and the south. These were the natural combatants for space. Then there were the people. They were the poor, the many different folk of the Tribes for whom the old ways were no longer good enough or strong enough to meet their wrenchingly small demands for a piece of the pie they believed they smelled cooking in the government offices in Bagui. They camped where they could, in structures of cardboard when they could not find wood or tin sheets. How they survived each day Fasseke did not know. Why their torrents of hate had not yet reached him he did not know either. But surely they were there. What they'd expected, with every right of the wretched, had had to go north and even beyond the sea.

Things took time; more than he wanted them to. There had been changes: Fasseke had carried his nation through six years without the tribal genocide the Franklins themselves had fomented to maintain power; through his health programs, supported by WHO, every man, woman, and child in Pandemi now lived three years longer. They did not care, of course, Fasseke knew, because they did not *know* these things. They would have to become self-evident.

Fasseke spread his legs and distributed his weight. It was time for the lights to come on. This was the moment he wanted to share with no one, though the cabinet had pushed for a massive celebration. Now the lights started to come on, a section at a time. There, *blink!* There, *blink!* And there, there, and there, *blink! blink! blink!* Later, Radio Pandemi would play his taped message, but Fasseke knew that a few new streetlights satisfied none of the Pandemi expectations. This was a start. There would be no more outages as there were all over the continent (save South Africa) when ancient machinery first built by foreign companies cresting the Industrial Revolution, and willed with unctuous graciousness to Africa, kicked off without warning, hurling Pandemi back into Conrad's Africa. Now there was power. Power and its by-product.

There came a soft knock on the door.

"Come," Fasseke said without turning. He knew the visitor was Nmadi Ouro. He heard the carved ebony door swing open and he then turned to see Ouro entering with a backward glance at the security men.

Fasseke signaled for the men to close the door and he walked across the room, his hand extended. "Come in, Nmadi."

Ouro walked carefully toward Fasseke; he walked as though he were a tall, uncoordinated man. But he was average in height and weight for a Grebo man. They shook hands. Fasseke thought he'd put on some weight. He found himself almost pleased to see Ouro.

"Mr. President," Ouro said.

Fasseke wondered whether he should ask Ouro to call him by his first name, as in the old days. Instead, he said,

14

"Nmadi. Good to see you again. Are you putting on a little weight?"

"No," Ouro said. "Are you? The politician's life agrees with you?"

So that was the way it was going to be. Years ago they had decided—at a party in one of those awful Notting Hill flats—that Pandemi had had enough of politicians and needed statesmen, thinkers. "Like you," Ouro had said then. They were students at the time, as tough and as sound as brass lifted from the mold and dipped in water. Now Ouro seemed to imply that he was, like most of Pandemi's presidents, just another politician.

Fasseke gestured to a seat. "Sit down, Nmadi. We can't have Pandemi's and perhaps Africa's greatest poet standing around. Poets outlast presidents. Sit down, man, sit down."

Ouro sat. He scanned the view through the window. It was splendid with the dark coming on fast. Did Fasseke appreciate it? Had he time for such things now? So much had happened since the West African National Secretariat and the West African Students Union had convened a conference in support of Pan-Africanism in London at the end of August twenty years ago, when the names flashed like gold beating back the sun: Du Bois, Hayford, Nkrumah, Danquah, Marryshaw, Azikiwe, and Makonnen and Kenyatta from the East. . . .

"I'm glad you came, Nmadi," Fasseke said. "It's been too long." He smiled at Nmadi Ouro, upon whom age was mounting its ambush at the corners of his eyes, the sharp little lines at the edges of his mouth, the fine, clean wrinkles in his neck above the collar that seemed far too tight and hot for him. Yet Fasseke was somehow pleased and saddened

---

15

both that his old friend had worn a suit to their meeting. Fasseke wondered if he seemed to have aged as much in Ouro's eyes.

"Had I a choice, sir?" Ouro asked it coyly.

Fasseke grimaced. "Not much. That's true. You've been raising so much hell that I'd have turned over all of Africa to get you here."

"Dead or alive, Mr. President?"

Fasseke absorbed the words as though they were blows. He fought them off with anger. "Nmadi, stop behaving as though this were another country and I another man. You cannot name a single person who has been exiled, killed, or suppressed since I've held this office, not even, mind you, a poet!"

Fasseke was pleased that his anger seemed to have made Ouro wary. But it was not good this way. He said, "Did you see the Green Flash today Nmadi?"

Nmadi Ouro smiled for the first time. "Yes! I did! You too?"

They grinned at each other.

In London while students they had talked about the Green Flash; it made Pandemi seem closer, made London bearable, and it made them feel superior. Why would nature waste a Green Flash over Brighton or Dover?

Ouro studied Fasseke's face. He had admired—still did in some coldly objective fashion that did not sit well with his emotions—Chuma Fasseke. He had seemed to be what Pandemi needed to wrench it out of its contradictory posture, which was half in the present and half in the past. Ouro had supported Fasseke when a replacement was sought to pull

---

16

the country back together after the Franklins departed six hours before an angry band of Chopis and Sothos sought a serious conference with them. And Fasseke had been a good man, son of a long line of ironsmiths who, like a pantheon of lesser gods, traced themselves back into the past of Pandemi, indeed, *African*, history.

When a student, Fasseke, like Ouro himself and a few others, had refused the generous aid of the mining and rubber companies that were still intensely raping Pandemi. The Franklins had not liked that, but Fasseke's father had made some money with the rubber. Ouro's father, through means Ouro himself did not know, had secured for his son one of those "save the savages" scholarships to England, where the two had met.

Of course after the Franklins, Fasseke had had to nationalize the foreign companies; that was expected. And he'd had to make deals, but hardly anyone seemed to know which kind. That he had dealt with Shaguri's Temian was certainly a far better bargain than many another nation was striking these days. But, Ouro reflected, Fasseke had let grass grow in his compound, something no good chief ever allowed to happen. Expectations small or great had vanished as a gust of wind. There were always excuses. Pandemi stagnated.

Ouro wrote about this in poetry, in articles, in books. He was uneasy about his eager and immediate acceptance in the West as a "perceptive analyst" of the African scene; he remained uncomfortable. But his lineage demanded that he tell stories. That lineage was long and receded even more deeply into the past than the ironsmiths'. Who had told the stories to entertain the smiths while they worked? Who had

17

kept all the family, clan, and tribal histories in their heads, histories that burst forth in week-long recitations during the festivals or when other important events took place? Surely Fasseke had not forgotten his, Ouro's, heritage. Was that a danger to the president? For the first time Ouro felt nervous. It was true that people had not vanished during Fasseke's regime, but would he be the first? Why had he been summoned to this well-guarded, tightly secured office?

Nmadi Ouro almost jumped when a man far too large to be just a waiter appeared at his side. "Would you like coffee, tea, or a soft drink, sir?"

"Ginger ale. Please."

The man vanished without a sound and Ouro said, "This looks like a very serious meeting, Mr. President."

Fasseke barely was able to conceal a chuckle. He had seen Ouro start. "Very serious, Nmadi," he said. "But I'd like to know what you're working on these days beside me."

Ouro found himself smiling. There was still something of the old Chuma in the man. "Another"—and here he paused to laugh silently at himself—"epic. Pre-European history. Traffic between East and West Africa, language connections, similarity of customs—"

"Excellent!" Fasseke interrupted. There were always the old tales, relationships, continuities as with any peoples on the same land mass, but Africans rarely did anything about them; too many Europeans standing in the way. "Do you know this fellow Diop in Senegal?"

Ouro was pleased. He felt the excitement he always felt when exchanging ideas with a sincere and knowledgeable Africanist. Why had he forgotten that Fasseke had been

interested in nearly everything? "I don't know him person-
ally, but I've read most of his work."

"Fascinating studies," Fasseke said, as though he had not
heard Ouro, who was reminded that he, too, was that way
when it came to ancient Africa. "I understand," Fasseke
said, "that the French gave him a tough time before they
reluctantly gave him his degree. First level too. He's supposed to have defended extremely well." Fasseke leaned
toward Ouro. "Must you call me 'sir,' Nmadi?"

The big waiter returned before Ouro could answer. Ouro
took his ginger ale.

"I'm just waiting for Pendembou to join us," Fasseke said.
"Then we can talk. It's very important that we talk."

The moment had passed, Ouro knew, when something
they'd had between them had been recaptured; the time,
distance, and office between them made as nothing. It was
gone. Ouro had heard of this Pendembou, Abi Pendembou
from the East. Chief of staff. Chuma's right-hand man.

"I'm flattered that you take the time to talk to a poet," Ouro
said.

Fasseke grinned. "Maybe presidents should take the time
to talk with poets instead of with other politicians. Of course,
Churchill was different; he believed he was a better writer
than Shakespeare. And Kennedy, poor man, wanted to be
seen at least once with a poet, and de Gaulle has his Malraux,
only sometimes poetic, and Senghor *is* a poet and so must
seek his own counsel."

They were laughing when the knock sounded. "Pendembou," Fasseke said. Abi always knocked. "Come in, Abi,"
Fasseke said.

19

The door swung open to admit a slender man in the traditional Pandemi robes. He inclined his head toward Fasseke. "Mr. President," he said.

"Abi," Fasseke said with a gentle wave of his hand. "This is Nmadi Ouro, our poet and an old student friend."

Pendembou came across the room, his robes whispering, his sandals slapping softly against floor. He smiled and held out his hand to Ouro. "The griot of griots," he said. "The storyteller of storytellers. Mr. Ouro, it's good to see you here."

Ouro had risen. Pendembou's hand was long, thin, and soft. He had a small, angular face and penetrating dark brown eyes.

"A chair, Abi?" Fasseke knew that Pendembou never sat in his presence.

"No, thank you, sir." He remained standing, a case under one arm. To Ouro he said, "I've read all your works and I have liked them very much."

"*All* of them?" Ouro asked. He glanced at Fasseke.

"All," Pendembou answered. "Maybe I will sit down, sir."

Fasseke, surprised, nodded. "An unexpected pleasure to at last look at you on the same eye level. It seems that poets bring out the best in us."

"Or make us tired," Ouro said quickly.

Fasseke was gazing with pride at Pendembou. Tonight he sits down, he thought. Pendembou liked to observe rank, status, place, lineage. A true African. All matters of state passed beneath his hands or were carefully scrutinized by his sharply slanting eyes, that roving, needle-sharp brain. He missed nothing and no man in the cabinet was at ease in his presence. Pendembou, too, had gone to college in America.

Like Fasseke, he had returned home shortly before the Franklins left.

"The truth is," Pendembou said, "there are some of your works I did not like, but I could understand why you wrote them."

"Ah," said Ouro, wishing for another ginger ale or something far stronger, "the truth comes out. I'm glad you understood the reasons behind them." Ouro shifted in his seat. "But now, Mr. President, I *am* curious about your asking me here."

Fasseke slid a glance toward Pendembou, who said, his voice as pleasant as before, "You forget yourself, Mr. Ouro. You do remember that we were taught to wait until the message is told to us."

Fasseke waved again. "He's impatient, Abi. He reads about America—Watts, New York, Birmingham, Selma, Montgomery; grows impatient about our leadership. This has been helped, naturally, by an ego grown large through publication in distant places. Modesty, always an attraction in the Pandemi people, even under the Franklins, sometimes is overwhelmed." Fasseke paused to smile at Ouro. Ouro thought it was a sad smile. "Remember, Abi, we are about to offer our brother a vision of the Pandemi future, one of justice, which cannot be bought cheaply. It is a vision he's long sought for all of us. His impatience may be due to that."

Ouro watched Pendembou nod as if in acquiescence, fold his hands; then he looked at Fasseke.

"Nmadi Ouro," Fasseke said in a less soothing voice, "whatever your limitations—and we all have them, even you—you're important to Pandemi, whatever it is now and whatever it will be. The people listen to you. They read your work. They think. They grumble. You talk of our future and that's good, because in any nation in which poets do not talk of a future, none will surely occur.

"When you're not writing or reciting poetry, when you're not writing your articles, you talk about the roads, the schools, the tension between the tribes, the failure of this government to live up to its promises. We promised to try, Nmadi, and we have done things—until tonight not evident— that we hope will ensure a future in which we can do all things. It is not your fault for not knowing; it was never the way in Africa to tell all things to all people. So when you asked when we would have elections, a question that suggests that I am a dictator leading our people down a dark and terrible road, we were upset. But we understood. We'll never travel the same road so many other leaders in Africa have traveled. In any case, you may recall that democracy was formulated above the tin mines where slaves worked. In Greece."

Fasseke paused and Ouro, feeling a chill creeping along his spine, working its way up toward his head, managed to glance without expression at the window; he marveled that he could not see where the ocean ended and the sky began now that darkness had come.

"I asked you here to explain the past six years," Fasseke said. "I wanted you to know where so much money and planning have gone. I want you to understand that I have been trying to guarantee a future for our people. That has been costly."

"Please," Pendembou said, "respect this confidence for the time being."

"Of course," Ouro said.

Fasseke said, "Nmadi, we have begun operation of a fast breeder nuclear reactor. You've seen the new lights, and were you at home right now"—Fasseke glanced at his watch—"you'd be hearing my address, which I taped earlier, on the radio. What I did not say was that we have every intention to convert the waste product into materials for nuclear weapons."

Ouro for the first time heard the waves crashing out on the beach.

The wind had shifted and Fasseke was starting to feel warm.

Abi Pendembou checked his fingernails. They needed cutting.

After a long pause Ouro said, "The West Germans?"

Pendembou and Fasseke smiled at each other. Ouro was suitably impressed.

"No," Fasseke said. "Who is not important, is it? We've come to despise ourselves so. Why not—Africans?"

"That surprises you?" Pendembou asked. He was grinning.

Ouro acknowledged the mockery of his tone with a rueful smile. "Where?" he asked.

"Oh, you've probably already guessed," Fasseke said.

"Jija Deep."

Fasseke and Pendembou smiled at each other as though to say, You see?

Ouro got up and walked heavily to the windows. He was not sure he liked knowing this, not sure he wanted to be involved in this "telling" session. "There has been talk," he said. "There is always talk." He paused. Neither Pendembou nor Fasseke spoke. "A bomb? Bombs?" Ouro said without turning.

"We cannot stop them, we cannot bargain with them without such a weapon," Pendembou said. "It's all they understand. Without the agreement between Kennedy and Khrushchev that followed the Soviet removal of the missiles, Cuba would have been overrun long ago."

"We have been under surveillance by the Americans since we began," Fasseke said. "From sea and sky."

"Jija Deep has everything," Pendembou said. "It's isolated and it can be defended. There's fresh water for the plant and it is not that far from the Temian border. Mr. Ouro, they do not want to see the manufacture and storage of weapons north of South Africa, you understand that?"

"Yes." Ouro said it with a sigh. Of course he knew it. But he asked, more plaintively than he wished, "Are we ready for this?"

Fasseke shrugged. "We didn't produce these conditions, Nmadi. And we have support, though you'll never hear of it publicly, from other African nations."

"Not Shaguri, though, I'm sure." Ouro spoke with disdain.

Pendembou laughed. "Especially Shaguri."

Ouro regained his seat. "*Shaguri?*"

"Oh," Fasseke said, "he plays their game very well. Does that surprise you?"

Ouro nodded. He looked at Fasseke with more respect, then he stared across the room to the window again.

"What are you thinking, Nmadi?"

"Of Du Bois. If only he'd lived three years longer! To have seen this . . . "

Fasseke and Pendembou remained silent until Ouro turned to them. "But why do you tell me this? To write of these things?"

"No," Fasseke said. "Because I want you to join the cabinet. To replace Griffin as our ambassador to the U.S. as well. We left him there to reassure the Americans that we would behave after the Franklins. Even after we nationalized, it gave them some sense of continuity for him to be in Washington. But now they know that we have a game too. He can come home."

"They have sent us one of their old liberals," Pendembou said, "and we would like to send them one of our new nationalists. *Literary* nationalists," he added. "You know the U.S. far better than we. We looked up at it during student days; you have been an honored guest many, many times. You might even be able to persuade some of our brothers and sisters to come and live and work here."

Ouro looked up quickly.

Fasseke said, "They're feeling the fire over there—again. This might be the right time."

"You're not afraid of what Nkrumah was fearful of?" Ouro asked. "The reasoning behind his banning of the African edition of *Ebony*?"

"No, Mr. Ouro. I don't believe our people are jealous of the African-Americans or their Cadillacs and closets filled with fine clothes. We've never marked their leaving by showing off old slave forts; we have Jija Deep, which will outlast all the slave ports in Africa. What foolishness is it that says we should continue to ignore such a rich variety of skills they have? Aren't they, with all their problems, among the best-trained black people in the world?"

Pendembou waited to be challenged. None came.

Ouro took a very deep breath and slowly expelled it. "You know, I'd just about given up. I didn't think it would ever happen, this kind of thinking, the cooperation, the nuclear activity—a start toward true independence. . . ."

Fasseke nodded. It was true. After Ethiopia, Pandemi was the second black independent nation in Africa—the first republic. Pandemi had been independent for 119 years. These other nations, Fasseke thought, had only to look at Pandemi and see how this western-style "independence" worked when it was handed over by someone else, not won in the heat of battle, the flash of fire. True, Pandemi's independence was a gift from another age; perhaps not as much a gift as a way out of the old American problem.

The land had been purchased from the reluctant French and British, who wanted no black republic between the regions their Mungo Parks, Hugh Clappertons, Paul du Chaillus (a black man who passed for white), and Louis Bingers had claimed for them. Set between two grinding colonial powers, Pandemi had been allowed to linger like a struggling flower on a rain-forest floor. It was a flower that had been ill tended by the former slaves turned masters who had been returned to Pandemi. The generations had witnessed their American attitudes of caste and class, their making the English language into the official language. They had been the new tribespeople with their American names and silk hats, striped pants and swallow-tailed dress-of-state. They had closed their eyes and palmed the payoffs from the foreign companies until the day they ran. Independence meant to them nothing. But now Nmadi Ouro had said it: true independence. Good.

Fasseke stood. Pendembou stood. "So, Nmadi, do think about the proposition." Fasseke embraced him. Ouro embraced him in return. Ouro shook hands with Pendembou. "When shall I let you know?"

"Tomorrow afternoon," Fasseke said. "Is that time enough for you?"

"Yes. Quite enough."

Fasseke knew he would go directly to his father's home to discuss the parts of the talk he could reveal. Fasseke knew he would have done the same, and so would Pendembou.

The big waiter came. "They have seen the new sections lighted up, Mr. President, and they've heard your address— and the people are cheering." The man gestured toward the window and they all moved to it.

"Yes," Pendembou said. "I hear."

Fasseke and Ouro smiled at each other. "I have to go now," Ouro said. The big man went out behind him.

When the door closed, Pendembou asked, "Will he do it?"

"Yes, I'm sure he will. Nmadi's always liked challenges; he's always wanted what we wanted. You know, Abi, I think he truly believed I was going to have him killed. For a moment I thought I saw that kind of fear in his eyes. Just for a moment. And that is precisely one of the things we have to begin to change about all of Africa. Now," he said, suddenly overtaken with weariness, "what does the evening briefing hold?"

He hated the evening briefings; all the accumulated rot of day came with them and they sat like hot stones in his stomach. The briefings were barriers between him and his wife. They had so little time together. The rot simmered in his sleep, made their lovemaking brief, exhausting rituals. The morning briefings were less irritating, if he had managed

27

to get a few hours' sleep. Or maybe it was the bright sun promising as it did every day new beginnings.

Tonight, however, Fasseke looked forward to Pendembou's briefings. Pendembou was opening the python-skin case. One or two pages fluttered as if by magic in his hand. Not so bad, Fasseke thought.

"President Shaguri advises that, as you requested while you were in the north today, radar watch has been extended to cover Jija Deep and the adjoining borders. His Blue Squadron is now on permanent alert, and communications are now established between General Obika and General Kehinde."

Shaguri's Blue Squadron was manned by pilots who'd trained to fly the fighters (they were American planes) in the U.S.—Randolph, Goodfellow, Connally—Fasseke could not remember all the names Shaguri tossed around with great familiarity. The man was playing his part well. Speechmaking like the dutiful puppet, but behaving with the cunning and wisdom of a bush doctor. Like Nkrumah and Selassie, Shaguri dreamed of a united Africa.

"The deep-sea fishing fleet," Pendembou was saying, "reports that the *Belmont* continues its mission." Pendembou smiled. "Watching for Soviet missiles. How can the Americans insist on that canard without being embarrassed?"

"The Americans," Fasseke said, "are never embarrassed; awkward, yes. And arrogant. Africans are not supposed to know that that rusting old ship has all kinds of electronic gadgets on it, or that their satellites know almost as much about Jija Deep as we do. Thanks to certain friends." Fasseke laughed. "So we have the edge because both sides know what we have and will get, and it'll be damned awkward for the West to try to dismantle our plant."

"Didn't you just suggest, sir, that being embarrassed or awkward was not enough to stop them?"

Fasseke glared at Pendembou. "Okay, Abi. Is that it?"

"No, sir. The new military attaché arrived on the afternoon flight."

Fasseke was made curious by the tone of Pendembou's voice. There was a teasing quality to it. "Is there anything unusual about him, Abi?"

"Well, yes, sir. He's a major and an African-American."

Fasseke turned from Pendembou's impassive face to the window. The stars were very bright out there above the sea. "A major," he said. "Once they were all first lieutenants or captains, and all of them white. Now a major who is black." Fasseke traced the structure of his cheekbones with his fingers. "When I was a student in the U.S., I often thought that a black man posing as a janitor in one of those supermarkets could cut shoplifting tremendously. Who would believe that black people would ever be empowered to make arrests?" He laughed in a low register. "Obviously the Americans think we have a supermarket here and have sent in a janitor." Fasseke turned back to Pendembou and searched his eyes. "It's Jacob Henry, isn't it?"

Pendembou nodded.

TWO

"Jacob! Jacob Henry you say?"

Fasseke's father seemed to chip the name out of the heavy, fragrant night air. "Ah, it's been so long. Ho's a soldier still? Uh-huh. Like his father?"

"No," Fasseke said patiently because he had explained it before. "The Reverend Henry just wore a soldier's uniform, remember? He was a chaplain, a man of God who saw to the needs of the soldiers. *Jacob* . . . was . . . *is* a real soldier."

"A killing soldier, did you not say a long time ago? I do not forget everything, my son."

"Yes, then, but not any longer, I'm sure. It's been a long time since he went away to Korea to fight. He must have another kind of assignment, because there is no fighting here in Pandemi."

"But aren't the Americans fighting somewhere else now?"

Fasseke said, "Asia. Vietnam."

Akenzua said to his son, "The Americans fight the yellow people so much. Why?"

"I don't know." Fasseke's eyes were used to the darkness now and he looked around his father's compound. It was empty, of course, since no one lived in it. Uncle Bonaco should share this, he thought. The sky was oddly, beautifully, luminescent, more beautiful than Fasseke had ever seen it anywhere. He was comfortable here. Fasseke had not imagined that he, too, like Nmadi Ouro, would be sitting in his father's house this night. Pendembou's information was the cause of it. Jake was back at a curiously coincidental time. Perhaps Fasseke's father could retrace the years once again and in the process reveal something about Jake that Fasseke had missed. He had not always listened carefully to his father as he ranged down back the years when the Henrys first arrived in Pandemi as missionaries; he needed to know all there was to know, all he'd forgotten, all he'd never known. Fasseke sipped his coffee. His stomach grumbled. He had thought this would be one of the rare nights he'd spend at home with Yema, but here he was instead.

Akenzua was speaking. "I was surprised when the Reverend Henry came back, you know. Uh-huh! And that's why I remember more sharply *that* day than when he first came with his wife such a long time ago."

Fasseke leaned against a post. He saw the red glow from the cigarettes of the security people. They'd driven here through the section with the new lights.

"I wished you to marry the girl," Akenzua said. "She would have been married to a president who brings new lights to the country, who speaks on the radio often, like tonight."

Fasseke did not know how to respond to his father's great pride. He said, laughing softly, "I wanted to marry her myself." Fasseke knew he was going to ask. And why not? Hadn't he, Chuma, come visiting, seeking knowledge to fill in the gaps he was then too young to know existed?

"My son," Akenzua said gently. "What happened? What truly happened when you saw Miriam over there? Had she changed so much? When you were children she was like your shadow."

The sea was whispering against the beach now. Fasseke tracked the breeze, which was again picking its way inland in a soft, steady stream. "She didn't like Africans, Father. That childhood we had was dead. She accepted the possibilities her country offered. What else was she to do? And she invested her future in material things and in gaining high places because of them. I had nothing."

Fasseke felt his father's sadness.

"Did you go out together?"

In the darkness Fasseke smiled. After all this time, these questions. He was not sure what had made this possible, this intrusion, which at another time neither would have permitted. "Yes," Fasseke answered, "but nothing came of it."

"Ahhhhh," Akenzua said, and then fell silent. After a time he spoke again, arousing his son, whose ease in that place had almost lulled him to sleep. "I think, Chuma, that the Henrys suffered very badly when they left us and went back. That was what changed the girl. Bent further the boy. Changed the father."

"They did not seem to be as well off when I saw them as I'd imagined they would be—"

"How so? How so?" Akenzua broke in.

"It was nothing they said. It was the way they seemed to be living. They were too proud to tell me anything, Father. But the Reverend Henry, who was so important in our village, was a man without position or power when I saw him. He was the custodian of a great cathedral on the edge of Harlem—"

Akenzua broke in again, abruptly, with an edge to his voice that Fasseke remembered from his childhood. It was impatient, demanding, close to being angry. "What is custodian?"

Fasseke thought, a janitor, but said, "A sweeper." That his father could understand; there were sweepers all over Africa, men and women who cleaned up the day's waste.

Akenzua hissed. "But how did you know, why didn't you tell me?"

"I saw him one day, quite by accident, Father. He didn't see me. He swept the walks leading up to this grand place. I returned several times to make sure I wasn't mistaken, taking great care that he didn't see me."

"Oh, no," Akenzua whispered, but Fasseke heard.

"When I visited between studies they never talked of a church. They didn't even talk about religion."

In a falling tone his father said, "But Chuma, why did you not *tell* me?"

"I knew how much you loved the Henrys. I knew as a child. I didn't want you to grieve for them. What we despise here may have been quite all right for them there. . . ." Fasseke's voice trailed off. "I didn't tell you, Father, because I didn't want you to grieve for them. There was Mother, you know, who had died,"

"Yes, yes, I understand." Even in the darkness, with its strange light, Fasseke could see him shaking his head. "Terrible, terrible. I didn't know it was so bad. Yet—how could I have helped?" Fasseke heard something in the question, rhetorical as it was, that at least once must have been thought or voiced by every man made helpless by distance, ignorance, or lack of money.

Briskly now, as was his way when emotion must be dismissed and business settled, Akenzua said, "The boy, Jake, Chuma, he who, like his father once did, has returned. What about him then? Was he like his sister?"

Fasseke sipped his coffee and remembered the pain, the betrayal, he thought it then, that he had felt; the binding arbitration not set down in words, but in remembered acts, touches, sounds, had no longer existed. He recalled the bewilderment, the emptiness that assailed him in the presence of Miriam and Jake, who had become strangers; at times he still sensed the sad and pitying eyes of the Reverend and Mrs. Henry upon him. They'd understood.

"I believed then and now, Father, that Jake was pleased Miriam didn't like me. We did things together, Jake and I sometimes, and I went with Miriam to museums and for walks that somehow never led to serious talk. Jake taught me the black American talk, and we went to places where they played jazz music. Be-bop, they called it, and in spite of everything it was nice to be in New York instead of London, where there were so few black people."

"What kind of music is be-bop music, my son"

"The kind of music white people could not easily steal from black people."

"Uh-huh! Uh-huh!"

"The Reverend and Mrs. Henry were kind, but they couldn't change anything," Fasseke said.

"No," Akenzua said. "There are such parents, more today than ever." He was sad that his son had been hurt—even now it echoed in his voice. And he, Akenzua, had not even guessed at that hurt. However, he was glad his son had come, if only for a study of the past so he could work his way with the future. He was pleased as he gazed at his son through the darkness in which they were speaking so softly, as they should so as not to disturb the things that belonged to it.

"Jake," Fasseke said, "believed that his father was a weak man, that being a man of God made him weak. Jake despised his father. Jake joined the army to be strong. I last saw him before he left for Korea, and he was looking forward to it. To the killing; he was not going to be like his father."

"And now he is here. Jacob Henry." Akenzua sighed.

"Tomorrow or the day after he'll present his papers and ask to see me, and surely he'll want to see you too."

Akenzua grunted. He was not sure he wanted to see this man who'd come without doubt to do harm to his son. "Well, it was that place they went to when they left here that changed them, Chuma. They stayed here so long because he was to get a comfortable church when they returned. Ten years they were here. The boy and girl were born here. Our women, your mother, too, delivered them. Then they returned to that place of bitterness." Akenzua's voice took on the edge again. "The church they got was a shambles, the Reverend Henry told me, with few parishioners, who were very poor. His church conference would not help them. He had to work in a factory so he could feed his family. And he had gone to university!" Fasseke was glad the darkness concealed his smile. The Henrys had gone to a small black church college in the American South. You had to understand that nation in its late 1920s to understand what that meant in the way of education. Still, the Henrys had labored successfully to educate themselves beyond the church. Perhaps that had been the problem. But his father was huffing away: "Not like here! Back then, people who went to university were special to us; to *all* of Africa."

Fasseke felt his father's hand. They wrapped fingers. "The war had come to America," Akenzua said. "And Reverend Henry joined the army because he knew the army would take care of his family. He *told* me that, yes! There were some things I didn't tell you, Chuma, because *I* didn't want *you* to grieve. What," Akenzua asked of the darkness, "could one do?"

Fasseke heard his father swallow.

"That day," Akenzua said, "when he returned, I was at the forge. There came a stir in the village. I didn't know what it was about until someone came to tell me that the Reverend Henry had returned. Returned! I couldn't believe it, my son."

Fasseke squeezed his father's fingers. Some of this he'd heard before in the lightness of pleasant times, with the Henrys far, far away, locked and boxed in a past from which they'd never emerge. Now it was the present and another Henry had reappeared.

"Of course, we'd all heard of the black American soldiers in the month of June 1942. They were building things. The big airfield, still in use, that the big planes use; bridges, roads, big buildings for them to stay in. From time to time we heard about so-and-so's daughter who had been made pregnant by one of the soldiers; that there had been fights; that someone's son had run off to try to join the American army.

The soldiers were never in our district, so we didn't see them, only heard about them."

Fasseke was remembering the talk about the black men from across the sea who were American soldiers. All he could remember thinking was that all the Africans hadn't died when they were taken from Jija Deep.

"We had tried to keep up the Reverend Henry's church. You had to sweep clear the yard every week, remember?"

"Yes," Fasseke said.

"His conference sent no one to replace the minister; almost no one went there after the Henrys left. What for? We'd always had God, long, long before the Henrys came. Even so, one or two tried to conduct services, but they didn't do them like the Reverend Henry. So no one bothered to go to church.

"When he returned that day he seemed to be a stranger. It wasn't just the uniform with the little crosses on the collar; it was his face. A great bitterness had settled on it. You yourself pulled me aside and whispered, 'Father, he looks different.' I'm sure you don't remember."

"No," Fasseke said. He did not remember, but he must have been twelve or thirteen at the time.

"He brought that iron hat for you, and the brass from the big bullets they shoot at airplanes. And little cans of awful-tasting food. The people sang and danced for him. He didn't want to see his church. We didn't have time for the roast goat because he'd taken us by surprise, driving up like that in that funny car. And he had the fever too. That was what made him talk as he did, I think."

Akenzua clapped his hands softly, slipping them away from his son's, and briskly rubbed them together. "He talked of betrayal during his fever, of that terrible place where the church was falling down, of the bitter, bitter cold, and working in that factory. Ah! I can't imagine it! We gave him *mo a yidi* or *yini za* for his fever. He laughed one moment and cried the next. He could not understand why this, Pandemi, felt more like home to him than America.

"We offered him a girl, but he refused. A woman, and he refused, and then a boy, and he refused. He thanked us, but said no. He did not seem to be offended. That used to be our custom, in the old, old days, to make a stranger comfortable, and since he no longer was, truly was, a man of God, because his God had left him, he said many times, we thought he would be a man like any other. He refused them all."

Fasseke smiled. Had the Reverend Henry not been tempted by the woman? Well, he recalled, they were close, the Reverend and Mrs. Henry.

"He came out of his fever and returned to his camp. He visited once more, a year later. He didn't look at his church this time either. He said his army was going to Europe, and that his family had moved to New York. We never saw him again. But you did. The rubber and the war made all that possible. It was the rubber, my son, that started you along the trail that made you the chief of chiefs of this place." Akenzua chuckled and Fasseke heard the irony in his father's voice.

His father was thinking about the rubber and how great a change it had made in their lives. The rubber made working the iron less honorable. The white men were greedy for rubber, and their iron was coming already shaped in packages from the United States or Great Britain. The American company planted many, many trees and herded the people into ugly little houses nearby to care for the trees. The people became almost like slaves, living close to work, their children going to school to learn to talk about the rubber plants, the children forgetting the past and the teachings of Segbo and Mawu. Of course the Council of Elders tried to maintain the old ways, a belief in the ancient God and gods, the dignity of the tribe and all people, an order that was maintained by a tradition that began beyond memory. Most of it was futile; the people wanted the American money, the American ways.

But the council never sent men from the district to work as other councils in other districts did in order to appease the government and make a percentage from the workers' earnings. If the men wanted to go, that was all right. No one made them. The Reverend Henry had been proud of that, proud of us, Akenzua thought, and maybe that was why he got so little help from home. Poor, poor man. Then the war coming in Europe. Strange that it came just when it was time for the Henrys to return home after ten years. Those years now seemed far shorter to Akenzua than when they were actually passing.

In the darkness, his son breathing easily beside him, the sea hissing silkily against the beach, Akenzua recalled that that was the time when, with his brother and uncles, they'd planted twenty acres of the Datar 10 Hevea rubber trees— 2200 trees. The rubber company wanted that, and paid well for leasing the land. They also bought land outright and cheaply, too, because so many people wanted to sell it to them. Oh, the white men planted rubber trees as if they were crazy. Tires for the war, they said, for cars, trucks, planes; for the insides of this and the outsides of that. It was supposed to take five years for the trees to mature, when they were five inches around. But the white men wanted them tapped before that time, and double-tapped at that.

The family worked the trees, no helpers, no poorly paid people, just family. At any other time the white men would not have allowed *that* to happen—but they needed that rubber. There was very little time to work the iron and there were times when he wanted to do so. Brass was impossible to get and the fact that the Reverend Henry brought some that time still moved Akenzua. But now Chuma was speaking, bringing him back to the present gently, as though he, Akenzua, had not slipped away into the past and was reluctant to return.

"Jake had a way with people, Father. It wasn't charm. It was calculation that I came to see. All wrapped in a bright, precise smile. When I talked of African independence, of Africa for Africans, he didn't seem to understand. He was amused. He was tolerant. It was as though those ten years we shared here were nothing. His mind was on other things."

A particularly stiff curl of wind set the leaves to clattering. The voices of the security guards drifted to Fasseke. He imagined they were as tired as he.

"He was always a child who needed a victory," Akenzua said through a yawn. "It was good he had you for a friend, Chuma. He laughed at the other Pandemi boys if he thought older people were not around. He bullied those he could. In the village there were always people who saw things. There are moments when you perceive in a child a thing out of place that you may not be able even to name. It just *is* out of place, and you know it will always be with that child. That's why we do not name children until they are a year old. We think then we can see how they have been shaped."

"I remember that you liked Jake, treated him like my brother."

"For you, not for him, though one must always be ready to love children. Always." Akenzua paused. He moved even closer to his son. Their thighs touched. "What is it that you do that brings Jake like this? Surely not this thing about the new lights and the power station? His coming has brought you here to talk down the night. His coming has not made you happy. And he comes without first writing. What is it that you do, my son?"

"What we do is what all of Africa must do, Father."

"It has to do with the lights and the power, those things going on above Jija Near?"

Fasseke chuckled and rubbed his father's back. Uncle Umoja. He still drove a wagon from Bagui to Jija Near and back, sucking up gossip and talk and jokes all the way. "It's"— he paused—"atomic power, Father," he said, concluding that that was a more familiar, a more limiting image than "nuclear power." He stood and his bones snapped, one in his back and one in his knee. Beyond the treeline in the east, daybreak was lightening the sky. "And we must have it."

"Just to be modern?"

Fasseke was saddened by the wistfulness of his father's question. "No. Am I not your son?"

"You are," Akenzua said, "my only son, and so I know there is more to this than you tell, maybe because I won't understand."

Fasseke pulled his father to his feet and slipped an arm

41

around his waist. He was surprised at how thin, how light, his father's body felt. "Do you remember when you used to say, as your greatest grandfather used to say when there was a big thunderstorm—"

"There is," Akenzua said, "all the anger of the gods let loose."

"Yes, yes!" Fasseke said. He squeezed his father to him. "They are fastened inside that power station. But we can let them loose, to roam where we direct them to go. And they do not want that."

Akenzua jerked inside his son's embrace. "They? They? Who is they?"

Fasseke could now see something of his father's face, long, narrow, black; the cheekbones protruding, the skin caved in beneath them. "The same that were greedy for rubber; the same that carried the old ones from Jija Deep across the sea; the same that said Segbo and Mawu were not as powerful or as good as their God. Even now they watch us with things I do not know or understand because they don't want us to have this power."

"The white men."

There it was, boiled, burned, down to understandable essences. Fasseke squeezed his father's waist again. It still amazed him that he could look down at him; he didn't now remember when he'd ever had to look up at his father, but, of course, there had been that time.

Akenzua sensed that his son was trying to take his leave and said, "It was good of you to come. I know you're busy. It was a good visit, but I wish you'd wanted something to eat. It's not good for a man not to eat."

"I'm all right, Father," Fasseke said, loosening his arm.

"Give my regards to your wife." Akenzua refrained from asking if Yema had become pregnant yet. Every man, no matter how busy, no matter what his station, had time to see to that. Akenzua followed his son to the edge of the porch and watched him walk slowly into the circle of men who were always with him.

Akenzua watched the small caravan of cars roll away into the first rays of day. He wondered if he had been able to give his son some armament to blunt the threat that Jacob Henry's coming posed. Jacob, of course, was a member of "they." Chuma had not had to say that. Akenzua sat down. There were things Chuma had not said, things he'd talked around. He always, Akenzua did, felt great pride when Chuma came to visit with his car followed and preceded by other cars filled with big men with roving eyes. The neighbors, of course, would have seen too. Nosy bunch. Always wondering why he did not choose to live with his son and daughter-in-law and enjoy the good life a president's father surely could afford, even here in Pandemi. Chuma's infrequent coming did at least let them know that it was his decision, not his son's, to live alone quietly. Back in the village they would understand that.

Akenzua twisted. He could feel his bones pressing against the wooden bench; his flesh had melted away, where, he did not know. His flesh no longer was the solid warm cushion. He looked seaward, following the sound of the fishermen who were already putting out and singing greetings to one another, just as they'd done forever and forever as far as Akenzua knew.

He closed his eyes. It was strange that the Henrys kept returning to Pandemi, like Digitara or Emma Ya circling the

Dog Star, to pull and tug at their lives here in unseen ways. Akenzua stretched, yawned, and went inside his house. He heated water on the propane gas stove Chuma had bought for him, and spooned out some of the American instant coffee. His cup filled, he returned to the porch again, noticing that the air was growing heavy with the smell of burning charcoal and of foods being prepared for breakfast. Now and again a voice wafted delicately against the morning, a woman, a man, a child wailing softly. *They*, he thought as he drank the coffee.

"They." It had always been "they," from the time of his grandparents and beyond. And not all white either. How the Franklins and their friends danced for the Americans in their silk-black skins, with their talk of republics and democracy, and this and that, God thrown in to clinch their arguments. How were we to know, Akenzua asked himself in his exhaustion, "we" being all those who'd come before him and those who'd come with him, we Kru, Mandingo, Kpwessi, Gbandis, Mano, Grebo, Gio, Ge, Gbundes, Loma, and the rest, that the Pandemi-Americans had established a new kind of government in the land in those days? A commonwealth? What was a commonwealth? Share all the wealth? A republic? Were these better than the federations the Pandemis had always known?

Akenzua had believed that when the Franklins went, all that had gone with them. He considered once again that they had not gone to America when they fled; they went to Europe instead. Curious, curious, he thought. When they went, Chuma became president; he was thought to be the best man among those who knew, those who'd gone to college, had walked the outside world. Akenzua had moved to the outskirts of Bagui because his son wanted him there. No family was left in the village, but Bonaco between trips, was near. Things did seem to get better, Akenzua recalled, and then worse. Akenzua no longer looked forward to trips back to the village where he had once been praised as the father of Pandemi.

The sun was now beating its way up above the trees, and Akenzua's corrugated tin roof, a new one already blazing in the sun like polished silver, was starting to pop and moan as it expanded. Akenzua kneaded the joints of his long, thick fingers. When he was teaching the young ironworkers, it was hard for him to grip the tongs or hammer now; his wrist weakened quickly. He thrust out his hands and spread his fingers, studied them. Wearing out, he thought, as all parts of all men do.

He dropped his hands. He wouldn't go to the council forge today. The boys who came were few and only half interested in the tradition anyway. (They were always forgetting to apologize to the trees, and to ask forgiveness for cutting the wood from them in order to make fires for the forge.) No. Today they could sell fruit or pepper to the whites, who seemed to spend every day lying on the beach. He would go to Jija Near, ride with Bonaco, and try to get to Jija Deep and look things over. Akenzua went inside and stuffed a change of clothing into a plastic bag. Bonaco would be leaving from the marketplace in about an hour if his schedule had not been disrupted by the pleasures Bonaco so often found with young women. Bonaco was but two years younger than Akenzua. Bad business, Akenzua thought. If he'd come and live with me, he'd have to behave.

Akenzua paused suddenly to wonder at the momentary

45

out-of-body sensation that overwhelmed him without warning; he waited for it to pass, as it always had. Was this the way of death? He had considered the feeling before. How light, how bright, how very, very quiet.

He knew that his daytime slumber had become too sweet; it enticed him to remain as he was, great, great distances away from all things. And his night sleep always revealed to him new trails in strange lands while offering up old riddles in new shapes and altered answers.

The moment passed, though he knew the time would come when it would not. Akenzua hurried. He had not made a trip north in a long, long time.

THREE

The wagon was painted crimson, lime, and gold, the colors of the Pandemi flag. It bore across its hood the legend NOW A PEOPLE IS COMING. The wagon was laboring up the slight hill spewing thick blue fumes. The people inside were talking loudly as they shoved and elbowed for room; the running boards were filled.

Jake Henry watched from the terrace, where he sat smoking. He was still tired from the trip and had not slept well. The growling air conditioners had not helped either. This section of Bagui, he thought, was more European than African, and that mammy wagon down on the street was a stranger prowling through a part of the city that disowned everything the NOW A PEOPLE IS COMING stood for. Jake didn't remember even hearing of the city when he was a boy; they'd never left N'Duli. No way, he thought, could Bagui have been what it now was.

From the corner of the terrace he could just see the servants quarters; they were arranged behind each complex of buildings like the garbage sheds behind the houses in Amsterdam, New York. Jake remembered that because he'd run across their low tops, scaring rats. He did not recall much else about that time, and he did not try to. That was in another life, neither here nor there, an ugliness in limbo. Nor did he want to remember too much about Pandemi right now; yet, its colors and smells assailed him, forced him into the past from which names now drifted up: haemanthus shrubs with their huge red balls of flowers, the hibiscus, and the faint scent of pepper. Remembered and recognized. Some recall begun, he looked once again at the name on the wagon. Where from . . . Then came the leakages of the past, more steadily now, the Bible lessons, his mother's arm swinging up and down in a teacher's rhythm, the young voices calling to each rising, Genesis, Exodus, Leviticus, Numbers (pause), Deuteronomy, Joshua, Judges, Ruth (pause), First Samuel, Second Samuel, First Kings, Second Kings, First Chronicles, Second Chronicles (pause), Ezra, Nehemiah, Tobit, Judith, Esther, First Maccabees, Second Maccabees (pause), Job, Psalms, Proverbs, Ecclesiastes, Isaiah, Jeremiah, Lamentations (pause and heading for the home stretch), Baruch, Ezekiel, Daniel, Hosea, Joel, Amos, Obadiah, Jonah (faster now), Micah, Nahum, Habakkuk, Zephaniah, Haggai, Zechariah, *Malachi!*

Then his mother's smile and the passing out of the little gold stars to be affixed to a card. The name on the wagon was from Jeremiah, Jake thought with a smile of self-congratulation.

Now a people is coming from the North
a mighty nation;
from the far ends of the earth
great kings are stirring. . . .

Why would I remember any shit like that, he wondered.

Coming from the quarters now was Dawson, the man he'd been introduced to last night. Dawson, the marine driver had told Jake, was his houseboy; Dawson cooked, cleaned, answered the phone, washed clothes, shopped, ran errands, looked after things. Had been checked out, of course. Had worked for embassy people before. Was okay. Dawson looked older in daylight. He walked almost without body motion, and Jake recalled that was the way the people walked, to avoid extreme exertion in all this heat. Dawson, Jake thought as the man moved out of his sight. Names. The old American input. Nineteenth-century back-to-Africa movements. Repatriation. Dawson, yes, indeed. Franklin. Brown. Jones. Smith. Yet, look at them. They were about a minute better off than when their great-great-great-grandpappies had their asses snatched into the boat. Maybe 400 years of slavery would have helped them. At least they'd know which end was up. Yeah, it was easy to tell who had been in charge of *this* place, Jake thought. No more slave descendants now. The *old* blood ran it, the traditional blood, Chuma's folks from out of the bush.

NOW A PEOPLE IS COMING had stopped to squeeze on more riders. It started off again, pursued by a man who was clutching an awkwardly wrapped package. He tried to force his way on to the running board; the passengers protested and pushed him away. The man persisted, jogging beside the wagon. Jake wondered just what space the fellow thought he could find on the vehicle that was already so loaded that its pan scraped against the roadway with each bounce. The man pleaded, and every few feet faked a dash on to the running board, a movement that increased the intensity and volume of protest from those already aboard.

An old man leaned out of the passenger side of the driver's cab; an old man who looked exactly like someone's uncle or father or brother back home, Jake thought, a man who was startlingly familiar, a person vaguely but nevertheless annoyingly remembered. The old man said something to the intruder, who then retreated from the still slowly moving wagon. He stopped and turned his backside to the passengers and, dropping his package, slipped his short pants down. He bent his naked backside and slowly moved it from side to side. The passengers roared, laughed and pointed. The man laughed too. The NOW A PEOPLE IS COMING groaned away. The man dragged his package to the side of the road and sat upon it, waiting, Jake supposed, for another wagon.

Jake heard Dawson in the kitchen and called out, "Morning."

Dawson came to the terrace, a great smile rippling across his face. "Morning, sah. You sleep all right?"

"Okay," Jake said. "What's for breakfast? Got bacon? Eggs? Coffee? Toast?"

Dawson nodded vigorously. "Yes, yes. American food. Delivered from embassy stores yesterday, sah. What you like, that bacon, eggs, toast, coffee?"

"Yeah. Please. Scramble the eggs."

Dawson said, "Okay. Chop come very quick, majah."

Jake lit another cigarette when Dawson left him. There were a few more people now walking along the street, and now and then a car drove by. The man was still sitting on his package; he seemed to be sleeping. He'll never get ulcers, Jake thought. He heard the bacon frying before he smelled it. He'd feel better after some food. He wondered what tribe Dawson belonged to. Not Mandingo or Mano; not Kru. Maybe a Chopis? Sothos? One of those, anyway, that had had close ties with the Pandemi-Americos. The name gave that away, of course. The embassy naturally would hire the Americos first, whatever the tribe they might have become attached to. The historical connection formed a firm enough bond. He wondered again what his life would have been like if there'd been no African slave trade.

"Don't you like it here, son?"

His father's tone, Jake remembered, was always slightly reproving, yet mildly sympathetic and tinged with longing. "It's all you've ever known."

No, Jake thought. That had not been true. He'd learned of America because his parents talked about it, had many pictures of places there and of people; they'd had books about it. It was a shining place that then seemed as distant but somehow as close as the skies all around him. "We will be returning; America is our home," his father had added. That had given Jake the sense of being a visitor who was always on the way back home, and had formed in him a curious detachment for Pandemi and everyone associated with it.

But now he was back, he reflected, back after spending more time out of the place he had been so eager to get to than in it. Still, he was usually glad to be posted abroad—even if he was equally glad to return. The last visit had been necessarily brief, just time enough to get Valerie and the kids settled in Silver Spring, which had just started to open up for nonwhites, and a quick trip to New York to see his parents and to tell them that he was doing what he thought might be a short tour in Pandemi as the military attaché. They'd been embarrassingly delighted. And why? Pandemi had been their Waterloo; nothing had turned up right for them since. There'd been no time to shop for gifts from them to Chuma and his father, Akenzua. But he promised to bear to them greetings and fond memories. Then the flight here.

Seeing the woman in the Pandemi terminal reminded Jake that for the first time in a very long while he would be on duty without his wife. She had said upon being told of the new posting, "Pandemi? *Africa!* Well, Jake, you *know* they don't have decent schools there, except for South Africa, and those are for whites. I hear the PXs have nothing much, and there'd be nothing to do, even if we found schools, except to hang out with embassy people. I can't stand them, and you know it; they're worse than army people. I'm trying to cut down on the drinking, and that doesn't sound like the place where that's going to happen. Jake—*you* go. It'll do the kids good to go to school at home for a while. These Germans are getting to be a pain in the ass anyway. The kids *need* good schools—let's hope there're two or three left at home with all this ruckus going on. I need to be with some real black folks, darling, and I don't mean in Africa."

Jake had not protested.

The woman in the terminal had caught everyone's attention. It was not only because of her size and bearing or the European air she seemed to have about her; it was the complete attentiveness lavished on her by a well-groomed young man and a uniformed assistant. Customs officers grinned and bowed them through. The uniformed assistant browbeat and lorded it over the baggage handlers, who were in a sweaty desperate search, obviously for the woman's luggage. The woman was Iris Joplin and Jake had seen her perform in a number of clubs in Europe. To Europeans she was the mid-century Josephine Baker, a more or less permanent Ella Fitz or Sassie Vaughan. She had to have come down in that Air Senegal 707 parked out on the strip; maybe, he had thought, a Paris-Dakar-Bagui flight.

What, he had wondered, was she doing in Bagui? He'd not heard anything about clubs. Was she just "doing" a part of Africa, the way so many black people were starting to? And who was the guy? Too young for her, but what the hell. Show biz . . . She had turned to catch him observing her and she smiled; Jake smiled back.

After she had left the terminal, all sturdy legs and steady stride, the uniformed assistant perspiring under the weight of her bags and the young man, side-vented tails swirling around him, deferentially leading the way, a big white boy, hillbilly type, Jake had concluded at once, introduced himself. They'd gathered Jake's luggage and flashed through customs with diplomatic papers and climbed into an American car.

Jake preferred the hillbilly boys to the streetwise blacks; the hillbillies were for God and country and did what they were told, showed respect, at least in his presence. The black soldiers brought all that historical baggage, unvoiced questions, and defiance at the conspiracy of events that had delivered them to the service of a sleeping God and a country that routinely demonstrated its lack of concern for them. For good duty at a quiet post, Jake had thought, give me the hillbillies.

Sergeant Coates was the driver's name, embassy detail.

Dawson called and Jake started in to breakfast. He thought that Coates and the others, whoever they were, probably felt the same way about Africa as he did. Was that why he was already feeling a sense of superiority here that he'd never felt in Germany? So far, he'd found none of the questioning gazes or offhanded manners that were always present when he was on assignment with Europeans or Americans. Here, he reflected, he would not have to wrestle with the secret uneasiness that had afflicted him all his career. He sat down. (The eggs were rubbery, the coffee weak, the toast hard, and the bacon still heavy with fat. Valerie, I'm missing you already.)

This place could be a nice change from the usual: family, army parties, detached assignments for USANEPU. . . . But he had yet to be told what the assignment here was. Obviously something to do with Chuma Fasseke and his government; it was in the record that he had been born here and knew the man who now president. In Europe, it had been the usual stuff: what're the Soviets doing? The Brits? The French? The West Germans? (For none of them could be trusted, a point driven home at all times by direct reference, innuendo, and inference too. We ran the game. It was our ballpark and our ball and we lent out the gloves.)

In Europe he'd been only a link in a complex chain which, he presumed, was used mainly to bind up the Soviets. If he'd been effective there, and he thought he had, it was only because the Europeans, only somewhat less than the Americans, discounted that effectiveness because he was black. But they used that blackness.

Jake glanced at his watch. Fifteen minutes before the car came to carry him to the embassy. There he would learn what was going on and what he was supposed to do.

"Dawson!"

Dawson peered out of the kitchen. "Sah!" His eyes questioned Jake's tone. "Breakfast okay, sah?"

Jake threw down his napkin and stood up. "No, man," he said. "Tomorrow cook the bacon *longer*. There was too much fat on it."

Dawson's face registered concern. "Not good? Cook longer, sah?"

"Yes, cook it longer, but the toast not so long and the eggs not so long, okay?"

Dawson smiled. "Okay, sah. You back for lunch?"

"No," Jake said. He expected to be at the embassy for the rest of the day. Coates had given him a schedule. Jake lit a cigarette. "And put more coffee in the coffee, Dawson."

"Okay, sah," Dawson said from around the corner in the kitchen. His voiced seemed sullen.

It was very warm, on the way to getting too hot, and Jake knew he was going to be uncomfortable in his uniform. He started to sweat just thinking about it. He walked to the terrace. There were many more people on the street now and the man with the package was gone.

The word around Washington was that Ambassador Woodrow Smallwood Fullerton was an ADA-type liberal, with ties back to Roosevelt, just barely, and a kind of a loose fit for the Kennedy-Johnson-style liberalism. Definitely not in the Bill Attwood, Ed Korry, Soapy Williams class. Harriman, of course, was in a class by himself. But the party owed Fullerton for both service and contributions. Nearly all the African countries wanted white, not black American ambassadors, and so here he was in Pandemi instead of Italy or Spain.

Yet there was a sturdy ambience in the blue-carpeted room; the place, its air conditioner humming, exuded confidence, and the ambassador looked like the old cartoons of Uncle Sam. He was tall, and his eyes were bright and alert, like those of an eagle. And his nose was hooked—broken while playing football for Brown, it was said. His hair was rumpled and gray-white. He'd been in the post two years.

"I'm glad to see you here, Major. We've fought a long time to make this possible. I understand this is your first embassy posting."

"Yes, sir," Jake said. He was standing at attention, his hat properly tucked between his left side and left arm.

Fullerton's eyes raked Jake's double row of ribbons and smiled. "No reflection on you whatsoever, Major Henry, but you may know that I've had reservations about having a military attaché here. I thought Gilchrist would not be replaced. I had specifically requested that. Pandemi has a 5000-man army, you know. And this is the only country in Africa where democracy is closest to the American model. Or was . . ."

Jake had not known about the ambassador's reservations. Evidently they didn't matter worth a damn to other people in Washington.

"Oh, I know it's still a mess in the Congo—er—Zaire—and conditions cannot be forgiven in South Africa; I know there are problems in Mozambique, Angola, Guinea-Bissau, Rhodesia, and that Fasseke has not held elections since he took over from the Franklins. Growing pains."

"Yes, sir," Jake said. "There's a lot going on over here."

Fullerton continued as though he hadn't heard. "Things here move slowly, and don't need to be complicated by military matters. But we are on excellent terms with President Fasseke, whom you know, I understand, and I propose we keep it that way. When did you last see Fasseke?"

"It was back during the Korean War, sir, fifteen years ago. But I was born here. Father was a missionary. Spent ten years here. Later President Fasseke came to the States to study."

Fullerton smiled. His teeth were yellow. "How does the son of a missionary wind up in the army?"

Now Jake smiled. "My father was an army chaplain, sir."

"There *is* a difference, Major. Well, never mind. I have to level with you: I don't buy this business of looking into the feasibility of trying to create an African NATO—or pulling Africa into the European alliance."

Why, Jake wondered, does this sound so limp? But he said, "Sir." The word was just to let the other person know you were listening; it did not offer an opinion.

"Just who would we—the Pandemis—be fighting, anyway, Major?"

They really sold him the cover, Jake thought. All right. The man was pissed because they hadn't listened to him. And Fullerton had bought nineteenth-century, not twentieth-century ambassadorial prerogative. Maybe bullshit. Jake hadn't met anyone in his life who had been serious about Africa, black or white. He decided to play it out.

"It's not the fighting or just the fighting, sir, but every country ought to have a well-trained army. We can instill discipline, teach contained area tactics, and these could be taught to the police."

The look Fullerton shot him revealed more than Jake thought was in him. In it there was disdain, perhaps even contempt, and it was similar to the glances that had come his way when superiors let him know that yes, they were aware of the Gillem Report and Truman's agreement with it. The ambassador said, "I know all that, Major Henry. Sit." Jake rested his hat in his lap.

"What these people need," Fullerton said, "are decent trade agreements, fair exchange for their exports, mineral and food products; sincere recognition that they are a part of the world and not an appendage of it. If we did for them just one percent of what we do for South Africa, we might be doing a proper job. So much of the money invested down there is used wickedly, and that NATO money we give to Portugal translates into arms, many of them ours, that kill the people who should have overthrown the Portuguese long ago."

Jake remained silent. Had Fullerton ever said these things to Gilchrist or to any other white person here on his staff? A younger, more ambitious man would not be saying these things. In Washington he was dismissed with a wave of the hand or a grimace as somehow not being a part of what was the real program. Fullerton spoke: "Sometimes it's hard being a soldier, I know, whether in uniform or not." He smiled and Jake thought he saw in it the kind of fleeting regret that teachers often cast upon students who revealed only briefly a kind of promise.

"Sir."

"Well," the ambassador said, pushing himself up with his hands on his knees and extending his hand, "once you get really settled and meet General Obika and devise some kind of arrangement, we can lay on a schedule of briefings, say, weekly? Gilchrist was pretty loose about it." Fullerton seemed to drift, then to collect himself. "It's a rather out-moded army, you know, but I'm sure everything will work out for us, Major. Your knowing the president will be helpful, I'm sure."

Fullerton was already walking to his desk. Behind it, he pressed his fingers against it, just as Jake was saying, "I hope so, sir." The ambassador's secretary opened the door to show Jake out.

"But now I suppose you see Ken Klein," the ambassador said.

"Yes, sir. That's on the schedule," Jake said. So, Jake thought, he at least suspects. Poor bastard.

They had driven, the two to them, from the embassy to this little restaurant that looked like a middle-class Pandemi house, one of those designed by the Italians. In the car Klein had said, "What say I call you Jake and you call me Ken?"

Jake had said okay and then they'd driven mostly in silence. Jake did not like Klein, but did not know why. And he was sure Klein did not like him either; he thought he knew why. It happened sometimes on assignment; personalities, however, were not supposed to clash enough to get in the way of an operation.

The restaurant was on a hilltop and it overlooked the sea. Soft, insistent winds made the place cool and pleasant. The food, which appeared on neat little oval dishes, was good, better than anything Dawson would be able to put together, Jake thought. The restaurant manager was a Lebanese. He kept emerging from a shaded corner to ask if the lunch was good; they assured him that it was marvelous.

"Fullerton's a nice guy," Klein said over coffee. "Really nice, but he's an amateur diplomat. Just right for this place. All humanist. No sense of the real world."

"They told me it would be a short assignment," Jake said. He was not going to get into any discussion about Fullerton. Fuck Fullerton. Fuck Klein.

"No, it won't be a long assignment, Jake,"

"Good." Jake did not like the certainty in Klein's response that this would be a cut-and-slash operation and out.

"Don't you like Pandemi? You lived here."

It sounded like an accusation to Jake. "I was a *kid* when I lived here." Why was it that none of them seemed to understand that? In the silence that followed in which Jake knew that he had communicated to Klein his open dislike of him, Jake thought of Fullerton and tried to imagine him as the ambassador to West Germany or France, Great Britain or the Soviet Union. In those places he would not have been ignorant of what was going on; he would have been a part of the machinery. Jake supposed the rules changed in Africa. Here, he thought, we do what we wouldn't dare do anywhere else in the world. He considered that and discovered he was wrong. Kennedy had fucked Stevenson. Before the entire world. Forgot about *that*, he thought.

"What's here that we're interested in?" Jake asked. He'd done his own research. There was the big airfield, the crops, the iron in the north, so much of it that the needle on a compass went crazy, he'd read. Gold, but so difficult to get to that it wasn't worth digging out. The airfield so close to Temian with all that oil?

Klein did not smoke. He had winced when Jake lit up. Klein had reread Jake's file that morning—you were always looking for something solid to take shape between the lines. Each time Klein had read the files the blandness seemed too bland—too filled with the records of duties assigned and performed; too officially exact, and the letters of commendation a touch or two out of the ordinary. There had been a line or two about his involvement with Manfred Rotsch, who'd come from East Germany and had worked with Messerschmidt-Boelkow-Blohm, but that had led to nothing more than a period of routine surveillance.

The man was a proper soldier. Military Intelligence School notwithstanding. Army intelligence did not have and never would have the global intelligence other agencies possessed. *Major* Jacob Henry had been sent up to the major leagues for two reasons, the first of which was that he was black, the color of the other fish in this sea; the second was that he had known Fasseke and might be of some assistance in this situation. Jake offered, Klein reflected, watching the pale blue cigarette smoke drifting past, little to grasp, like one of those fleet black halfbacks of old who gave you a leg and just when you lunged at it for the tackle, took it back, leaving you with nothing more than a brief trip through space and a mouthful of grass. Klein had never liked those fleet black halfbacks. He played defense, and when you missed a tackle on the corner, everyone saw it.

Klein said, "Did you get a chance to listen to the radio last night?"

Jake assumed this was partly in response to his question. "No," he said.

He had checked out his apartment after meeting Dawson, poured himself half a tumbler of Scotch from the new stock of liquor, and settled himself in an almost hot bath.

"Last night," Klein said, "President Fasseke announced that Pandemi had put into operation a new power plant that would provide new electricity for the country and speed its growth." He paused and looked at Jake. He supposed it was time to hand over the playbook.

Jake waited. He'd already felt certain imbalances here. He couldn't name them or place them. The assignment itself? Returning to Pandemi? The ambassador being more than he seemed? Klein, who would have been an A-number one Nazi? Maybe this was the job he should have begged out of. Shit. Every job advanced you toward the eagles and then, if you were lucky, knew the right people, a star. Well, why not a star, at least? He ground out his cigarette. Suddenly he missed Val and the kids, even the fights. He threw a feint at Klein. "So, they built a dam on the Carrodobu." He snorted. "Big deal. We started to build a dam for the Egyptians. So what?"

Klein did not shift his eyes away from Jake's face; he had watched the fleet back fake his way out the backfield; had him coming all the way. Even though the dossier said nothing about Henry's having played football, he was big enough, even club football at City College. Klein laughed. "The 'gyptians aren't all that far from our national security interests."

"Umm," Jake said. "Neither is Temian, which is right on Pandemi's border."

"Yes," Klein said.

Goddamn white boys, Jake thought. Think you know nothing. They count on you knowing nothing. "Okay, Ken," he said. "What do we have here? You're the boss. Another Dornier-Messerschmidt-OTRAG deal?"

To Klein the question sounded like an order. He shifted in his chair. "No, Jake, not at all. What they have here is a fast breeder reactor."

For the second time since he'd ground out his cigarette, Jake reached for the pack and then withdrew his hand. "Oh," he said. "I see."

Klein leaned forward. "You know what they can do with that, don't you?"

"You mean beside providing power?" Jake started to laugh. *This cat is something else!* He laughed harder at Klein's frown. The Lebanese came out and smiled at them, then retreated inside. "All right, where is the plant?"

Tight-lipped, Klein said, "Jija Deep."

"Jija Deep," Jake repeated. *One of those places like Bada-gry, Elmina, and God only knew where else, from which the Africans had been shipped as slaves to the west. Wasn't sanctioned,* Jake thought, *the way Tarpur had been three years ago. Heav-y. Don't want spooks to have nothin'.* Jake found himself nodding slowly, as though the motion were to indicate that he understood this most difficult concept. "And they have the facilities for storing the spent fuel—and converting it?"

"Yes."

Jake looked out to sea.

"There was a policy decision not to do anything about it while it was under construction," Klein said.

"They thought the Africans would blow themselves up, right?"

"That was a consideration. But there was another. Your buddy has had a great deal of solid support from Shaguri. If he blows Temian's wad on Fasseke's plant, we could buy his oil cheaper, separate him from OPEC, which will become pretty strong in another few years. But at least that part of the assignment may be over quite soon."

Jake faced Klein squarely. "What do you mean?"

Klein grinned. "Shaguri may find himself without a government, or even dead."

"Oh," Jake said. "One of those."

"Then all that's left is for that plant to have an accident, and you can take off for back home in Harlem."

"I live in Maryland," Jake snapped.

"I know. Just a way of speaking."

"You guys all speak the same language, and I know it pretty good." Jake spat. "How did Gilchrist do?"

"Zip." Klein was glad to be back on the subject. He shrugged. "Obika doesn't like white people, that's the way it is. So now it's your turn. Fasseke's already got buddies: the Soviets, the Chinese, maybe the French, the Kenyans, Ghanaians, Nigerians—everyone who'd like to see us eat dirt."

"Africans've eaten it for a long time," Jake said.

They looked at the sea again. "What's this accident?" Jake said.

"About in place. Couple of details. Don't want it too close to the Shaguri thing."

"No. When will you brief on that? The accident?"

Klein stood and dug out some bills and peeled a few off the wad. "We got time, Jake."

Jake stood too. "I thought the briefings were up front. Well. Tell me, where do you go in this town when you don't want to eat or drink at home?"

"The American colony is quite close," Klein said. "A round of parties every week. We even have a section of the beach reserved for us, and an entire deck on the yacht that goes up to Dakar. Real close."

"No," Jake said. "I mean when I want to be a-*lone*—but not quite alone."

The Lebanese manager bowed them out. In the car Klein said, "The Ashumn Hotel. Food's okay. People passing through stay there. It's not far from your flat."

F O U R

"Do you have *any* idea when he will be here?" she had asked.

It would be so much nicer in this magnificent chalet if he were here. Since she'd come, the air conditioners had been turned off and the night wind, with an abundance of fragrances, sifted through the building. Oh, it was a luxurious place; she could not have imagined such a place in Africa, although, of course, she might have guessed they existed. It was dark when they arrived in the small, sleek caravan of luxury cars, but Iris Joplin sensed that the scenery during the day was as stunning—more stunning—than the chalet and the grounds that were now bathed in discreetly located night-lights. And the help was smooth, though she'd seen only the two people who took her bags and later served her when she dined alone. There were others, naturally: the two tough-looking men who'd opened the gate and peered into each car, the people in those cars who seemed to have vanished somewhere in the night, leaving the cars crouching like panthers. And there was the young man who'd met her at the airport, Manoah Maguru, to whom she was now speaking.

"He should be here soon, Miss Joplin. Very important things happened today in Temian."

"I thought we were in Temian." She sat down on the delicately brocaded chaise that fitted so perfectly into the alcove where they were. She showed a graceful calf and produced the long liquid sound of silk on silk as she crossed her legs. She watched Maguru's eyes follow the movement, then dart back up to her face.

Maguru gave a faint, formal smile. "There are affairs of state, miss, between Temian and Pandemi, between President Shaguri and President Fasseke, and those affairs cross borders, miss. We are presently in Pandemi." He turned slightly and Iris, following his eyes to the place beneath the bay window, saw for the first time a bank of blackness laced with little red, yellow, and green lights. Telephones sat atop the bank. Maguru saw her tracking his glance and said, "You see, we will know instantly when he's on his way."

"But it's late."

Maguru shrugged like a European and Iris smiled. She had met many Africans like Maguru in Europe, where they'd come to study following the war. They told beautiful tales of the continent which was vast, restless, and eager for the freedom from European control they were then demanding. Nearly all claimed to be sons of chiefs (she rarely met an African woman there), and they carried about them a romance of land and history. Also desire. So many of them thought she should sleep with them simply because they wanted to sleep with her. But she was then with Time, and his presence, at once brotherly toward them and proprietary toward her, forced them more into the postures of nationalists than of suitors.

Then there was Taiwo Shaguri. He arrived shortly after her break with Time, when she was on her own playing Art Simmons's *The Living Room* in Paris.

He came every night with two large young men; one was this very Maguru. And every night there were flowers from him in her dressing room with a neat little embossed card attached: Taiwo Shaguri. The cards never carried his title. And one night there was a note as well as the card, inviting her to dinner.

He spoke with a curious accent; it was very British with an echo of an accent that was completely musical, like the rising and falling cadences of a song. He might have been the son of a chief, although that no longer mattered since he was the president of Temian, one of the first countries to have been given freedom by the British. Iris had not known presidents. The dinners continued; his reserve continued, even when on rare occasions they quit the Right Bank for the Left for restaurants like LeRoy Haynes's. He would vanish and reappear, talking of meetings and trips to England and Temian, laughing at diplomats and red tape.

"You must come to Africa," he always said at some point during their time together. And once she said, "But you must have wives."

"Of course," he said. "Two. And you, *you* cannot be alone."

She found herself ashamed to admit that she was, but she also sensed that he would not believe that it was because she wanted to be alone for the moment, without the attachments and demands of relationships like the one she had with Time. Her career was what mattered. Why not tell him?

When she was finished she wondered why she'd felt the shame in the first place; it *was* the career that was important. Hadn't she told Time Curry that? No marriage, Time, career. Time thought they could have both; she didn't think so, and that was that. "A . . . friendship, yes," she had concluded, "but I'm not into anything more than that, Taiwo. I don't respond to demands; I like requests."

Then he spoke. He had not made any demands, and didn't intend to. There were his two ladies back home. Europe, to be frank, was one thing; Temian was quite another, and Temian in any case was his paramount wife. He understood perfectly, and now that he did, could she see her way clear to spending a few days in Antibes with him?

So it had begun and now she was here for a visit at his request. She had at last "come home to Africa." And there he was out there in the unending darkness busy with "affairs of state." Well, it was a vacation for her, a break between quitting Paris for a time to work in Amsterdam. She could use the rest. Iris stood. "Good night, Manoah," she said. She walked softly through the hushed house to her bedroom.

That was last night.

Now it was morning and she was walking beside the shimmering blue swimming pool. She saw that the place was located on a plateau among low hills. The heat already stung. Out past the cleared area with its gardens and concrete sidewalks, the cars were parked beneath the trees. The men who had manned them were stretching, the sounds of their voices rising and falling. There seemed to be more men and cars than Iris recalled from last evening.

She tumbled into rather than sat in a chair at the edge of the pool. She eased her sunglasses back up on the bridge of her nose. This, she thought, is all cool and neat, and I needed to get away, but without Taiwo here it ain't really movin' me.

The housewoman came out and placed a pitcher of iced lime juice on the table beside Iris. "Mum," the woman said.

"Thanks," Iris said.

"Yes, mum," the woman said, as she'd said when she served dinner, when she served breakfast, when she was just merely present.

Iris watched her saunter back into the house, wide hips flowing slowly back and forth beneath a white uniform. God, Iris thought, turning to her book, even the heat seems busy in this place. She was peering over the top of her book at the cars and the men around them. Those guys have guns, she thought. How many guns does a president need to protect him when he isn't even here?

It was close to noon when Manoah Maguru swept from around a corner of the house. Iris wondered if he'd been up all night; his face appeared strained. He had changed to slacks and a shirt that was open at the neck.

He smiled as he came near. "Morning, miss. Sleep okay?"

Iris lifted off her glasses. "Yes, I did. Any word?"

"The president's on the phone now and would like to speak to you?"

Iris carefully placed a marker in her book and stood. She followed Maguru back inside the chalet. He gestured toward her room. "You can take it in there."

"Well," Iris said when she picked up the phone.

But a woman's voice came back. "Miss Joplin? Please hold for President Shaguri." The voice was not an African's. Before Iris could reply he came on.

"Oh, Iris, my dear. You're here. I'm so glad, but I *am* sorry that I couldn't join you last night as we'd planned. Some . . . untoward events took place and continued until just moments ago and had to be handled. Are you all right, my dear?"

"Taiwo, I'm all right, and the place is lovely, but it's like being a prisoner with all these men with guns. Do you want me to be your prisoner, Taiwo?"

His laughter rolled and bounced. "What a marvelous idea, Iris. Oh, I would like that, to have you just for myself, and you could also sing to me alone."

"What do you mean 'also'?"

His laugh was a small roar which she interrupted. "That might be great for you, but it wouldn't do much for my career, Taiwo."

"I know, I know, I know, my dear. So let me make a suggestion for the time being. I have arranged for you to have the Aggrey Suite in the Ashmun Hotel in Bagui. The best hotel and the best rooms—"

"*When* do I get to see Temian, Taiwo?"

"Soon, soon."

"Jesus, Taiwo. You know I came to see *you* and *your* country. Your wives must be a helluva lot tougher than I thought."

"Iris," he said. The lightness had left his voice. "The problem is not with the wives, but with my esteemed brothers."

"Brothers? I didn't—" She broke off, recalling that he always spoke of other black men as brothers, and those of

71

Temian as *esteemed* brothers. She thought of all the cars outside and all the men and all the guns, the strained look on Manoah's face. "Taiwo, is everything all right with you?"

And now he laughed again. "Ah, yes, my dear. There is a little cleaning up to do, but I'm all right. Temian is all right. There *was* a clumsy little coup d'état. It was nothing. But look now, will you do that for me? Move to the Ashmun? Bagui is much like Accara—markets, small museums, you know, some shops and lovely scenery. It's *sometimes* all of a piece, Africa. There'll be people around for you to talk to, things to do—"

"I want you around to talk to; I want to do things with you."

"And we will do them, dearest. In another day or so. I want so much to see you." Now he sounded tired. "I wanted none of what happened, but I suppose it was predictable. It is all *right* now, I assure you. I'll talk to you later at the hotel. It is best you go. Manoah will take good care of you, and my friend, President Fasseke, will also be watching over you."

"Taiwo," she said. She sounded, she knew, like a character in a film, the character which is supposed to show great concern. "Please be careful. I don't know what the hell's going on, but be careful and come quickly. I mean quickly."

"Of course, Iris, my dear. Now return Manoah to the phone."

As she ran to the alcove, she considered that Taiwo's voice, brisk at the end, was like that of an actor stepping out of character. Maguru was sitting smoking. "He wants you, Manoah."

Maguru nodded and picked up a phone. He glanced at Iris and she understood the look to mean she should leave. She returned to her room and hung up, then went back to the pool, replaced her sunglasses, and sat down with her book.

Oh, shit, she thought. Yes, Bagui. Somewhere she could hit the clouds in a hurry, if need be. She sipped her lime juice and peered over her book. There seemed to be more movement among the men with the cars.

When she was led into the suite by the exhausted-looking Manoah Maguru, it was at the very moment when the sun was sinking beneath the horizon of the ocean.

"Oh!" she said, and stopped. There was an instant's greening of all the light in the skies. "Did you see that! What was that?" Filled with awe, she approached the windows, her head turned to Maguru for an answer.

"The Green Flash, miss." He was smiling. "Only God-given people see that, miss. In Temian we don't have a view of the sea, so we think the Pandemis who see a Flash—or anyone else—are lucky."

"Marvelous!" Iris said, then realized she had whispered the word. She turned from the window and saw the two bouquets of flowers, one of roses. Where, how, she wondered, had he managed to get roses just like the ones in France? She went to the second bouquet and plucked out the card and read it.

"Who is Chuma Fasseke?"

Like a cloud hunching over the sun, Maguru drew near. "Mr. Fasseke is the president of Pandemi and a close friend of President Shaguri, miss. It is a welcome."

"But there's a letter too."

"Yes, miss."

Iris opened the envelope and quickly read the letter. She

tried to supress the joy that was forcing its way into her tone. "He'd like me to have dinner with Ambassador Nmadi Ouro—tonight. Ouro knows my brother! He's the new ambassador to the U.S. Do you know him, Manoah?"

"Only that he's Pandemi's most celebrated writer, miss."

"Ah, so that's how he knows Ralph."

"If President Fasseke requests, miss—"

"At eight," Iris said, whipping up her watch at the same moment Maguru did.

"You have an hour, miss."

"Could you confirm for me, Manoah? The letter asks for confirmation. You know who to call. I'd love to talk with the ambassador, especially about my brother."

"Certainly, Miss Joplin." Maguru signaled and a man entered with her luggage and disappeared into one of the rooms. Maguru retreated to a corner and picked up the phone that rested on a table.

Iris walked slowly through the rooms of the suite. As with everything Taiwo did, there was a touch of the lavish about it. She wondered if Ralph had stayed in such a place or if he'd ever been to a chalet like Taiwo's. Probably not. He'd said she should find profound differences between the way black American males and females were treated. Yes, maybe, but she looked forward to meeting this Ouro. Hell, she'd have dinner or just drinks or a mere conversation even, with anyone who could manage not to make her feel cut off from the world, a trapped creature in a lush, exotic greenhouse where the foliage concealed nearly everything. She wanted air, winds blowing, gales.

She heard Maguru's quick, heavy footsteps. Oops! she

thought as she turned to him. "But President Shaguri . . ." she said. She'd forgotten. No doubt Manoah had noticed.

"President Shaguri will be late, miss. Again. And he offers his apologies once more. You'll have plenty of time to meet with Ambassador Ouro. I've just confirmed. He'll be waiting for you in the dining room downstairs."

He seemed to have been expecting the question about Taiwo, Iris thought. He knew on the drive to Bagui that Taiwo would be late, for he had not made any calls and had not received any. Only the one to Ambassador Ouro. "Late? How late, Manoah," she said firmly. "Is he all right?"

Maguru waved a disparging hand. A sneer appeared on his face. "They couldn't hurt him, Miss Joplin. Loose ends, that's all."

Iris thought just then of Normand. He was her agent in Paris. "Africa," he had said when she told him she was going. "You're going to Africa? When? What for? For how long? Look. Call me a racist pig if you want, but Africa's not for you. They'll despise you even as they use you. You think Europeans are bad? Just wait. I've been there, darling, from Algeria to the Congo and all the places in between. You'll be glad to return, just the way Dick was. Tell me again—for how long? Business, Iris, or pleasure? You're booked for Amsterdam, you know. In just three weeks. I hear you see an African president." He had grinned, baring square, dull white teeth. "Well, there are presidents and then there are *presidents*, yes? Don't let them destroy you. Africa was never your home."

"Loose ends," Iris echoed. She raised her shoulders in an exaggerated shrug. What can you do? it said; that's life, it said, so there must be another game elsewhere. "I've got to rest, Manoah. The drive was tiring—rushing there and suddenly having to rush back here. You understand. Where will you be staying?"

"I return to Temian right now, miss. You'll be all right. There are two women officers in civilian dress right next door. They're in contact with President Fasseke's people."

"Why do they have to stay? Do I need protection? Why? From what or whom?"

Maguru smiled. "They're just to see to your needs, miss. To run errands—"

"And to make sure I just sit and wait for your president?"

Maguru waved his hands in protest. "No, Miss Joplin. You're a stranger. You came as the guest of President Shaguri and he feels obligated, as would any man, to provide assistance and—yes, if you wish—protection. But, he'll be here. Patience. That's what Africa's all about, waiting."

Briskly Iris said, "All right, Manoah. Maybe I'll see you later or tomorrow or—" She shrugged again.

"Yes, Miss Joplin. Have a pleasant evening." He was out of the door as he spoke the last word.

Iris sat down on a couch. She was, more or less, alone again. An African brushoff? she wondered. First time for everything. But why had she suspended her reality when it came to Taiwo? What caused this need to hand over control of her life, however briefly, to a person and place she knew not well at all? Something to do with putting distance between herself and Time? Between what she had been at Sissie's death and what she wanted to be? What? Career, she knew, whatever she told others, was not everything. She'd never admit that to anyone, not even to Ralph (who in any case probably knew it wasn't, and who in some ways was more driven than she). Was it Africa itself, a kind of time warp that cast spells upon those who ventured to pass through it in the same way they passed through other places on the globe? Guilt, maybe; the search for a place where beginnings were commonplace and where anyone who was a black European or American really belonged, a plunging through centuries to home?

Well, whatever. Taiwo had seemed to be the African different from all those randy schoolboys. (Was he still different, but now a victim of events he'd not completely shared with her? If so, then he, not she, had of course built the distance, perhaps with an eye to vanishing into it behind a neat fabrication of those very same events. What did she know? How *could* she know?)

She started at the knock on the door. "Yes?" Iris got up and stood next to the door.

"Ebu Ansaya, miss. With Tuzyline Edubo. We were with Mr. Maguru, miss."

"Shit," Iris muttered. She opened the door. The two women stood there dressed alike in skirts and jackets. Iris recalled seeing them in one of the cars in the caravan, remembered the way they had looked at her, studying her face, her body, her clothing. The one named Ebu was solidly built, with a round innocent face. The other was taller, thinner, her face filled with angles. Both were young, mid-twenties, Iris guessed. They crept shyly into the room and shook hands.

"Ebu and Tuzyline," Iris said. "I'm Iris."

"Yes, miss," Ebu said. "Everything is all right, miss? We are next door, 802. Can we do anything for you?"

Iris's smile was bright. Girls together, she thought. The women smiled back. "Well, ladies, I have to get ready for a dinner downstairs." She started walking through the suite. The two followed, hesitating with each step. "There's the bar," Iris said. She rummaged behind it, found three glasses and selected a bottle of Scotch. She poured. Ebu and Tuzyline glanced at each other. Iris handed each a glass. "Drink, ladies." She waited until they began to sip. "You know," she said. "Men are shits."

The officers exchanged astonished expressions that Iris immediately perceived as fakes. "*Shits*, miss?" Tuzyline said. "Oh, do you say so!"

F I V E

Why does that guy keep looking at me? Jake nursed his drink and stared across the dining room. He avoided the glances of the man. The room was softly lighted. Most of the white-topped tables were occupied. In the dimness the cloths appeared to be stiff, but his own cloth was limp with humidity, even with the air-conditioning. There was something pathetically imitative of European restaurants about the place, with its heavy silver, flower arrangements, and thick napkins.

Jake assumed that the diners, nearly all of them white, were from the embassies or were business people. The PCV's couldn't afford this place, Jake thought. He'd ordered the chicken with palm nut gravy, palm cabbage, and okra and plantains. He hoped the meal would be good, for it was costly. He didn't want to regret not having stayed at home with a steak prepared by Dawson.

Jake's eyes this time hooked with the man's across the room. The man nodded. Jake nodded in return and then slid his eyes away once again. Probably recognizes a stateside brother, Jake thought mirthlessly.

Klein, Jake thought. He wondered how Klein's little coup next door in Temian went. He had not mentioned the U.S. ambassador in Temian, a black man whose pictures had run in *Ebony*. Jake wondered if the ambassador was in on the deal. You could never tell why or what for with people like Klein. Now Jake recalled Fullerton's tone when he'd said, "But now I suppose you see Ken Klein." He'd kicked out those K's as if they were objects stuck in his throat. Maybe, Jake thought, the old bastard was fooling everyone.

Neither had mentioned a Communist conspiracy as a rationale for anything; certainly Fullerton would not have; Klein should have—except that he was smart enough not to; wasn't necessary because the ground had already been turned. ("We can't let Africa go Red.") Said the same thing about Europe after the war, and the eastern half of it went anyway; same in Korea, to which he'd rushed like a hero, and when that was all over, the place was still divided—and still policed. Same in Vietnam, taking up the slack for the French. If there were no Communists, Jake thought, we'd have to invent them, create them so businesses would boom, politicians could get votes, and the military could stay in business. He'd played the game, for a game it became after they almost shot his dick off at Yechon. Fifteen years later and here he was only a major; hadn't even thought of Vietnam where people were signing up to go to get their tickets punched for promotion. He'd take the desk and float it the next five years and cash it in and hope for eagles, at least. It's been—it was—a good life for Val and the kids. Not as great as he'd hoped, but certainly better than the life he'd had as a child. He'd wanted that, *needed* that, to show his father strength, power, and the ultimate weakness of God. Yet Jake had felt uneasy and perhaps even saddened when he knew his father, without declaration, had limped away from the faith that had sustained him (and them) over so much time.

Jake wondered if Chuma believed more in Africa than in God. Chuma could have had it so easy; Chuma, whom he would see tomorrow. Could have gotten "aid" from us generous Americans (though it would have been just a fraction of what the Europeans got and were still getting) if he had just declared Pandemi to be a democracy when he took over, and not built his power plant. Chuma was stubbornly African— "Africa for the Africans"—and all that. Jake almost laughed. Most black people were happy to lay hold to some guns; not Chuma. He wanted the gun of *all* guns, the great rifle, the biggest boom. Shiiiiit, Jake thought. Chuma was *bad*. Not a dummy, stubborn as Gibraltar, straight-eagle in African style as anyone might *not* be able to imagine, Chuma had pulled something off, had flown in the face of power, and against the entire history of what that power had always done to people who did not share it, dared to build a challenge.

And now, he thought, watching the woman weaving her way between the tables, heads coolly spinning to watch her progress, he was here to teach Chuma a lesson that Africans should never forget: Do not fuck with Sam. The woman— God, she looked good—was, indeed, he saw as she sat down beside the man who'd risen at her approach, the same man who'd been studying him, the woman he'd seen at the airport, Iris Joplin.

"I've only just accepted the post, Miss Joplin, so I'm not sure that I feel comfortable with 'Mr. Ambassador.' Call me Nmadi, please, like your brother. I saw him last in Cairo, you know, or more properly, Gizeh, where the pyramids are."

She was a very attractive woman, Ouro was thinking, more European, in a way, than American. Perhaps an affectation that had become a part of her manner without her realizing it. "Scotch? Scotch it is.

"We just happened to meet in the dining room of the Mena House. Hadn't seen him since New York, and there he was. He was there for three days. A conference on pre-dynastic Egypt. Interesting because the Egyptians reject any suggestion that their civilization began in the south. Your brother's interests never fail to amaze me. Anyway, we could walk out of the hotel and up the hill to the pyramids. They were that close. And magnificent. And the Sphinx was there, too, of course. We talked as we went, usually early morning before the tourists came to offer themselves as victims to the camel drivers and the self-appointed guides."

The drinks came and Ouro asked if she would like to try some Pandemi food. He was gratified by her smiling acquiescence, and so ordered for both the land turtle, hot green peppers, and butter pear.

"The guides. They were like fleas pulling and shouting at the tourists, many of whom were white Americans who unceremoniously shooed them off. Most of the guides were black. At one point Ralph said to me, 'Nmadi, I want to prove to you that to many white Americans all blacks are the same.' 'How will you do that?' 'Watch.'

"We were dressed not at all like the guides, who wore

soiled caps and gowns that had not been white since the cloth was bought."

Ouro broke off to laugh.

"Ralph was quite well turned out, I recall. He wore a gray, black, and red madras jacket, neat gray trousers, and a blue shirt open at the neck. He was wearing those—those easy shoes?"

"Loafers," Iris said.

"Yes, loafers. Ralph walked to a white American man— steel-rimmed glasses, gray hair, pleasant face, a man who was dressed as much in the American fashion as Ralph himself. Ralph plucked at the man's sleeve and said, 'Pyramid guide, mastah?' The American shook his head and backed away. 'No, no guide. Get away, get away.' Frankly, I think Ralph *wanted* to be wrong, but he wasn't."

They had another drink.

"I know your brother has mixed feelings about Africa, but do you think he'd live here if given the chance? I ask because foremost among my tasks will be to recruit American blacks to come and live in Pandemi to help us. So when I learned from President Fasseke that you were here, I moved quickly— at his suggestion—to meet you."

"I'm glad you did because I am thinking of returning to Paris tomorrow if I can arrange it." Iris smiled.

"But—so soon . . ."

So soon, Iris thought. Seems like a week. She said, "That's the way it is sometimes."

Ouro wondered why, and why she'd come in the first place if only to spend a couple of days. Who could even begin to know Africa in so short a time?

83

Sensing that she'd perhaps said the wrong thing, Iris hastened to answer the original question. "I know Ralph likes to travel in Africa—he likes to travel, period. But he is very attached to his daughter, who's in the care of his ex-wife. Also, Nmadi, you'll have to admit that these days the place for a black playwright to be is in New York."

Ouro nodded. "I thought that might be the case." He was both relieved and disappointed. Chuma, he knew, wanted people with skills, the technicians who made things work. And Ouro himself knew that the best playwright in the world was not needed right now as much as a plumber. Yet, he knew and Chuma knew that black Americans, even of artistic stature, might very well attract the plumbers, simply because a cause cut across all class lines. He was disappointed because Iris's responses confirmed his own knowledge that recruitment was not going to be easy. He persisted.

"What about," he said, his eyes sweeping slowly across the room once more to come to rest momentarily on the man whose eyes at that moment were fixed on Iris, "those people in Europe who've found it not quite what they expected?" Even in the asking he knew futility. They were mostly opera singers, jazz musicians, painters, writers . . . no plumbers. No farmers. No engineers.

"I don't think so, Nmadi. Like me, they'd have nothing much to offer that would be helpful to you right now."

"Perhaps, though," Ouro said, "through people like you and Ralph we might be able to communicate more directly to others—" Ouro broke off as he traced Iris's eyes to the man across the room. "That man's an American, isn't he? Do you know him?"

The man Iris had seen at the airport was grinning at her; the grin was a promise of devilment—given opportunity—a grin of admiration as complete as any she'd seen, man to woman, on the streets of Spain. ("Bravissima fucka" Time had called that look.) "No, I don't know him. I saw him at the airport when I came in."

"Odd, isn't it," Ouro said, "how we recognize always that similar something."

"Nmadi, after a while it's easy."

"All right, Iris. He's an American. Embassy? Business? Doesn't look like a tourist, does he?"

Iris grinned back at the man across the room and said to Ouro, "Why don't we ask him over? You might be able to recruit him." It would be nice to talk to an American, she thought; it would really be cool, and this guy looks like he knows what's happening.

"Would it be all right with you?" Ouro asked.

"It would be fine with me."

To hell with it, Jake had thought as he squeezed between tables. I'm going over. What's he gonna do, kick my ass? Ha! Shit, I'm a fan, and I haven't seen anything like her since I got here.

She was smiling at him. So was the African. "Hullo," he said when he arrived at their table. "I hope you don't mind. I saw you at the airport the other night, Miss Joplin, and seeing you again, I just wanted to say hello. I've seen you a few times in Europe."

"Oh, how nice. Thank you," Iris said. "This is the new ambassador to the U.S., Mr. Nmadi Ouro."

Ouro rose and shook hands. He gestured to a chair.

"Please sit down. Mr.—"

"Henry, Mr. Ambassador, Jake Henry."

"Mr. Henry. We were just about to send a waiter over to ask you to join us, seeing as how you're an American too."

They settled in their chairs. "And what part of the States do you come from, Mr. Henry?"

"Uh, Maryland. Right outside Washington." He held a hand to Iris. "Miss Joplin."

"Good, good," Ouro said, watching the handshake. "The evening is filled with coincidences. But Africa is the place where they often happen. Will you have a drink, Mr. Henry?"

"Yes, sir. Thank you." Jake smiled at Iris. Ouro flagged a waiter.

"So you've spent time in Europe too. Business?"

He had to be a soldier, Iris thought. Those black soldiers in Europe carried themselves a certain way, like this man, like her former husband, Harry, may have after she left him in Germany. How to define it? Not young dumb and fulla come, as Time would have said, but maybe old, bold, and damn near cold.

"No, sir," Jake was saying to Ouro. "I'm in government, in the army. Now I'm at the embassy here. Military attaché."

Ouro laughed again. "Coincidence once more. We're both diplomats."

Jake grinned. Iris was older than he'd thought, but had that self-possessed attractiveness, however, that seemed to yield nothing to age.

"Where did you see me in Europe?" Iris asked.

"Jack's Jazz Club in Barcelona, The Living Room in Paris, and the Tivoli Gardens in Copenhagen."

"You get around."

86

"You were always great," Jake said.

"And I haven't seen her once," Ouro said. "Not once."

"Umm," Jake said. He wondered if the two of them had anything on. Didn't seem like it, but you never knew. Jake raised his drink in a salute. Ouro nodded. "To one more coincidence," Jake said. "I'm new to the job too."

Ouro raised his glass. He wondered why Fasseke would have need of the American military. He sipped and said, "I was just explaining to Miss Joplin that one of my tasks in the States will be to recruit American blacks to come live in Pandemi. Have you any advice for me?"

"Mr. Ambassador, the only thing I know about is soldiering."

"Well . . ." Ouro began. "Maybe—" He stopped. Perhaps such things were better discussed with Chuma and Pendembou, not a stranger. Things like a well-equipped, well-trained army taught by black American soldiers, an army that would behave itself, one that did not grow powerful enough to think it was better than a civilian government. . . .

Jake waited.

Ouro dismissed the topic with a wave of his hand and a smile. After all, he now thought, this Mr. Henry may have come here to do just that, Ouro thought, with the express purpose of ultimately supporting a coup. Henry was a black all right, but he was also an American. "Coffee?" he asked. He glanced at his watch. "I've got to run along, Iris. Are you quite settled upstairs? Comfortable?"

Iris nodded. "I'm just fine, Nmadi."

Ouro leaned on the table. "Listen. Don't go tomorrow. I'd like to talk with you again, about Ralph and about Africa. Why, my dear, you've barely seen the place! You *can't* leave

87

tomorrow. So I'll call you, all right? But if you *do* leave, call me an hour or so before you go. I can drive you to the airport, if you insist on leaving. Will you do that? I know Ralph would want me to be of assistance to you. How can you go without meeting my family, eh? He'd never forgive you. So do think about it." He extended his hand to Jake. "Mr. Henry, it was a pleasure. We'll probably see each other again before I leave for Washington. It would be helpful for me to talk with you."

"Yes, sir," Jake said. "Anytime."

Now Ouro said to Iris, "I really hesitate to leave you. The president arranged our meeting and I sort of feel that you're in my care."

"How sweet," Iris said. "There's nothing to worry about, Nmadi. There are two ladies over there at the corner table. My escorts. Besides, right here I have an American soldier."

Ouro smiled. "Yes. I suppose a couple of Americans would want to compare notes about Africa." The words came out more tartly than he wished. He deepened his smile to soften them. "Well, I'm off then. And I hope to see you quite soon."

Chuma could not have expected much from this meeting, Ouro thought. Just contacts, tribal loyalties called into play, but Henry and Iris belonged to no tribe here. Ouro arranged with the manager to have the bill charged and then left the restaurant, walking slowly, head down into the heavy, water-logged heat, deep in thought. A respectful voice called to him. "Mr. Ambassador, your car. Did you forget?"

"How *do* you like it so far?" Iris asked.

"Haven't seen much of it. Been busy getting squared away in my quarters and at the embassy. You?"

"I've seen very little, but I've been moving around a bit too fast for me. *That* I don't like."

"What brings you in the first place, if I can ask? I mean, I didn't have a choice. Vacation? Sure got good contacts. The ambassador, the two ladies over there . . ."

Snoopy sonofabitch, Iris thought through a smile. "The ambassador is a good friend of my brother. Nmadi may be the best-known African writer in the world. I don't suppose you've heard of him."

"Nope," Jake said.

Well, Iris thought, neither had I until Ralph told me about him. "The ladies over there are my friends," she said, inclining her head in their direction.

"Can I call you Iris?"

"Do."

"They don't look like the kind of friends someone like you'd have."

"I don't know what you mean by that, but we're in Africa and you can't always pick your friends, unless you're lucky, and I am lucky." She wasn't going to say anything about Taiwo and President Fasseke. Screw this cat.

"Are you leaving tomorrow?"

"I've been thinking about it."

"The ambassador's right, you know. You really haven't seen Africa, let alone Pandemi."

"Neither have you."

"I was born here," Jake said, watching surprise build up in her eyes.

"I thought you were an American."

"I am. Spent the first ten years of my life here and then we went back home. My father was a missionary. This is my first trip back."

There was something new in her eyes. Interest. She was interested.

"Where was back home?"

"Amsterdam," he said, and then, "Amsterdam, New York."

"Really?" I'll be damned, she thought. "I'm from up around there."

His eyes widened slightly. "Where?"

She told him. "Did you get *The Progressive Herald*?" she asked.

"Get it? I delivered it for a while. And then we moved to New York. The city."

"Pretty country. Upstate." She'd thought about that often in Europe.

"Yeah, it was." He hadn't seen much outside Amsterdam, but he sometimes had seen, on a clear day, where the Adirondacks began their slow gallop up the sky. Sometimes he confused that memory with the mountains of Korea.

The restaurant was thinning out, Iris noticed. Ebu and Tuzyline, backs against the wall behind their table, seemed to be almost asleep. "Was it nice here, growing up?"

"I think," Jake said, "I hated it. I'm not sure."

"Why, why would a kid hate any place he happened to be?"

Jake made his drink lap around the glass. "Because there was somewhere else that we came from. My folks seemed to miss that place."

"Still alive, your folks?"

"Yeah. Yours?"

"Father. And then there's my brother. He's younger, but not by much."

"An adolescent."

"You're sweet."

Jake glanced around. "Isn't there anywhere else to go? A club, a joint, something?"

Iris said, "How would I know? I'm a stranger."

"Maybe your friends over there know."

She almost started to say that they were as much strangers to Bagui as she was. She said instead, "In any case, I'm not up to any clubs or joints. I'm a little beat, Jake—"

"Don't go back tomorrow. Come with me to the village I was raised in. N'Duli. I gotta try and . . . rediscover myself. Come on. I can't do that with an African and I don't want to do it alone."

Iris hesitated.

"Air-conditioned car," Jake murmured. "Take a snack. Back by dinner . . ."

It might give Taiwo another day to get things together, Iris thought, if they needed straightening out, if he wasn't giving her the door. Why not? This guy seemed nice enough, although it was clear that he was after more than a drive, a snack, and pleasant company. Most men were like that. No big deal. She could handle it. What the hell. "What time?"

"About noon." Jake was seeing Obika at ten and Chuma at eleven. He'd have to rush home and get out of his uniform. "Deal?"

"Deal," she said.

"Nightcap?"

"No thanks. I've had a long day."

"It'll be nicer tomorrow."

Iris caught the challenge in his tone. She rose laughing from the table. "That's what they all say, Jake." She saw that Ebu and Tuzyline had gotten up too. Iris took Jake's hand, which he held for an instant longer than he should have, and she knew that he knew it. "See you tomorrow, Jake."

"Sleep well, Iris."

Jake watched the two women who were dressed alike join her as she walked past their table with a friendly nod in their direction. A friend of Ouro? Two lady bodies. Did Klein know and simply didn't tell him? A connection, and a sister at that. Fucking Klein. Fucking spyshit.

At about the same hour, Akenzua and Bonaco Fasseke, riding in the NOW A PEOPLE IS COMING, rocked and groaned with the wagon as it pulled into N'Duli in low gear.

"Ah! But I'm tired," Akenzua said.

"And you haven't even driven!" His brother said with a loud laugh. He drove into the square, pulled to one side, and beat upon the horn. "They're all pretending to be asleep," he said. "They heard us coming miles away." He pressed again on the horn and the sound echoed through the forest.

"Bonaco," a voice filled with caution called. "Is that you?"

"It's me," he said. "I'm tired and hungry and so is Akenzua."

Figures approached the wagon. "What, Akenzua too? You tore him away from Bagui?"

"Yes, me," Akenzua said, climbing out of the wagon. He was sure he'd never be able to make another trip like that, not in this life.

"Greetings, Akenzua. Greetings, Bonaco." They were surrounded by a host of people with vaguely familiar faces and guided to the guest house.

In the same place and unchanged, Akenzua saw. Good, good. In the light he recognized old friends and hugged them, asked of their children, their health. Quickly food and beer came and Akenzua and Bonaco sat down at the table and ate hungrily with their fingers, pausing to compliment the cooks and to ask of this one or that one. Bonaco did not include the village on his regular run and, while not the stranger Akenzua had become, he was not considered to be a regular visitor.

"We're sorry to disturb you," Akenzua said. "But I'm happy to see the old hospitality is sound. We have been north, where my son has had built a new power plant that has brought more lights to Bagui already. Soon there will be light in every village in Pandemi." He knew they were too polite to ask why it was that Bagui, which already had so many lights, needed to have more. The low chorus of approval was not sincere, but he continued. "We have seen this place for ourselves. You cannot imagine it."

"Big," Bonaco said.

"Huge," Akenzua said, flinging out his arms. He could not tell them that they'd had to sneak like thieves from Jija Near to Jija Deep, past all the soldiers, in order to see the place that could cause Chuma trouble. They would want to know why it was that a son held back from his father. They did not understand the modern world and how the white man behaved.

"Where is this place, Akenzua?"

Huuoop! Akenzua thought. Busy being the braggart. Careful. "It is a secret place," he said.

"Very secret," Bonaco said.

There was another chorus of voices, this time a pretended awe. But one voice, reedy, piercing, spoke. "Jija Deep is no secret, Akenzua." Giggles followed.

Akenzua and Bonaco exchanged a glance. "Does anyone work the forge?" Akenzua asked.

There was silence.

Akenzua swept up the last of the food in his bowl with a whisk and, shaking his head, said, "All the old ways are dying. One day, one day," he mumbled, for he was tired, very tired, and sleepy now that his stomach was full, "we'll all regret it."

Bonaco, near exhaustion, nodded slowly in agreement.

"Tomorrow," Akenzua said, "we'll talk more of the things my son is doing." He peered around, and then, moving slowly toward the canvas cot where he was to sleep, said, "You see the old ways are gone. Where is a woman for me?"

A soft OOOooooo sighed through the structure with its browned palm leaves, a sound of wondering and approval. This time the sound was genuine, Akenzua knew. Then he laughed and slapped his knee. "That is a joke! But, you see, the old ways are indeed gone."

There was another silence. Akenzua did not know if it was born of resentment or agreement. And then they left. Akenzua and Bonaco washed with water from the basins that had been discreetly placed beside their cots.

Bonaco said, "So, now that you know those buildings up there are real, what do you do?"

"Do?" Akenzua said, dipping the cloth, washing, wiping, wringing. "Do? Nothing. I have to think on it. Why must something always be done at once? Huh? To know is to know and very often that is enough."

"So it has been said, brother."

Akenzua finished his wash and fell on his cot. "Ah, but I'm tired, Bonaco. It was a grand trip though."

"Yes, it was," Bonaco said. "Imagine. My nephew did that."

"Yes, and you work as hard as you did before he became president. And do I live in an Italian house with servants? No. There are twenty countries in Africa where, if one member of a family gains office, all in the family gain office."

Bonaco yawned. "The way the Europeans did it, yes."

"Chuma seeks something else," Akenzua said. "Who would have thought it, Bonaco? Little Chuma."

Before Bonaco could answer, a series of snores raced out of Akenzua's mouth with surprising ferocity. Bonaco reached over and shook his brother, and the snoring softened. Bonaco sighed, blew out the kerosene lamp, and curled over into sleep.

S I X

General Obika reminded Jake of a sergeant major he'd once met, all laid back and cool, huge and smooth-skinned with the good life, the left breast of his jungle greens lined with ribbons. Jake knew that Obika had not been on good terms with the Franklins, which was why he'd remained a lieutenant until Fasseke took over. The Franklins' other military associates left the country when they did. Obika had paid visits to Sandhurst, Coetquidam, the USMA, and the War College. The visits to the States had been shorter than the others. That made him suspect. Obika had done a tour in Korea as an observer with the Ethiopians (while an aide to the Franklins' favorite general) and another in the Congo two years ago with the UN Nigerian troops.

Jake had arrived at Obika's office at ten straight up. He waited in the office of Lieutenant Mbundi. Mbundi's dress was neat, but without starch. He seemed to depend too much on his frightened sergeant; Mbundi was one of those men who invariably becomes, Jake thought, the eldest lieutenant on whatever base he's assigned to. Gray hair and gray stubble, a lined and resigned face, gave him away. He did his duty, chewed out his men, passed the buck. Mbundi did not seem like the kind of aide a man like Obika would have.

Obika apologized for the delay. "I'm pleased to see you here, Major. I would have thought that all the black officers would be sent to Vietnam." He smiled archly.

"Sir," Jake said, and waited.

Obika said, "It's a place where you either thin out the ranks or get promotion, right, Major?" He laid his palms down on his desktop. "It's taken a very long time for blacks to become officers in your army. And if Captain Gilchrist had his way, there wouldn't be any."

"Sir, there have been black officers in the U.S. Army since the Civil War. Nobody like Captain Gilchrist is going to change that. Vietnam doesn't matter." Jake hated discussions of racism. He found them more complicated to explain than he wished. This was true especially with foreigners. Such talk always left him feeling that he had defended, or tried to, someone he himself should have attacked. Now he was wondering how long Obika would have lasted had he been in the U.S. Army. Could he have cut the mustard like the three or four flag officers who were black? Jake resented Obika's short-rationed approach and conclusions. Shit, he thought, I know damned well that I know at least as much about the military as any four or five Africans in flag rank. Shit.

"I stand corrected, Major," Obika was saying with a smile. "Wrong history books. Wrong guides. You are in fact the first

African-American soldier I've ever spoken to. I know I've much to learn and I hope you'll be kind enough to help. Well, now, Major. This isn't exactly a hardship assignment, as you know."

"Frankly, General, that suits me fine."

"Our borders are quiet," Obika said thoughtfully, "and our army is small. Most of the weapons we have are from World War Two—I'm sure you know all this. But, you know, we don't go looking for adventures, as the Soviets would say. In fact, one could almost say that the army is ceremonial. You'll want to consider that if you continue with Gilchrist's desire to bring us into some kind of African NATO."

"Yes, sir."

"Nevertheless, you'll want to look around, so, next week, say, we'll lay on trips to the Greboland and Bacle Barracks. That'll give you time to talk over the old days with President Fasseke and visit N'Duli. It's not changed. The cities are always changing, but not the bush, thank God. The bush is the soul of Africa." Obika peered at his watch. "Time to get you over to the president, Major." He came to his feet with a bang. The sound was enough to catapult Mbundi through the door, where he stomped to attention.

"Get Major Henry to the president's office at once. Tell his driver to follow you."

Mbundi snapped off a salute Obika didn't bother to return and held out his hand to Jake. "Really glad you're here. I look forward to working with you on—whatever."

Jake saluted. Obika returned the salute. "Thank you, sir." Jake followed Mbundi out to the street, where he gave a nod to Coates, whose glance sought him out over Mbundi's shoulder. Intuitively Jake knew that Coates was taking no orders from blacks unless they were *his* blacks. Coates nodded back and Jake climbed into Mbundi's unmarked car.

Fasseke awaited the Jake Henry meeting with a variety of moods. The first was one of triumph for, after dispatching Ouro to meet with Shaguri's American lady, he'd hosted a cocktail party for the express purpose of receiving the congratulations of the resident diplomatic corps. Placating Shaguri's lady was far more important than having Ouro there to be introduced as the new ambassador to the U.S. It was Pandemi itself the diplomats were interested in, not one of its ambassadors. The party also gave Fasseke a chance to be with Yema.

So, they'd come smiling, the Americans, the Europeans from both the East and West, and there'd been the Africans and Asians and Latins, and they'd all smiled while their eyes searched the rooms for Shaguri. Fasseke knew he could count on the support of the Red Chinese, the Soviets, and the Cubans. The American's no, and the West Europeans, sometimes yes, sometimes no; many of the Africans, no. Fullerton wanted a meeting at the earliest possible instant; so did Hua-Ling and Karpinskov. The photographers had been busy recording the handshakes, the backslaps, the shifting groupings.

In addition to triumph, Fasseke also felt relaxed for the first time in days with Yema by his side, radiant as usual. And they had had the rest of the night together catching up on the "small news" and making love down the night. When he arrived at his office, whatever nervousness he'd felt vanished upon the news that all was well with Shaguri except for a few "odds and ends." Now Fasseke felt confident.

And Pendembou's morning briefing had brought word that his father was safe and relaxing in N'Duli.

Now Fasseke thought of Jake, the boy Jake, who'd been in his age group and learned the forests with him, the kinds of respect due to custom, older people, and the land they lived on; Jake, who, after sitting in his mother's schoolroom had had his education supplemented in the great Pandemi school: the bargaining in the marketplace, the ironworkers' forges, the rubber plantations, the Moslem chants, the names of the stars and winds, the time to plant and the time to harvest; Jake, who'd learned to burn a patch of wild grass on three sides and wait on the edge of the fourth to club anything that emerged from the inferno—turtles, bush rats, snakes—and then skin, gut, and cook them over fire; Jake, who'd watched old men, poems in patience, rhythmically chewing kola nuts while they took odd lengths of pipe, built triggers and sights, chambers and magazines, and wed them to ebonywood or mahoganywood stocks that'd been just as carefully carved and, finally, produce shotguns with which to hunt.

There had been no sign that Jake remembered when Fasseke last saw him on a visit to New York between classes at Syracuse. (There had been an unusual interest in Africa and Africans there, then, that seemed unduplicated anywhere else. Mondlane, among others, had been there. Yes! And also were there not contingents of blue-clad Air Force men marching from building to building, studying, it was said then, Soviet history and the Russian language?)

Jake the young man was nothing if not self-assured, even arrogant, for no reason that Fasseke then could understand. He had just finished college and seemed to be amused that

Fasseke was still going, albeit to graduate school. Jake was going into the army.

The Reverend and Mrs. Henry seemed to be appendages to, rather than forces in, the lives of Jake and Miriam. Fasseke sensed that they were not as considerate of their parents when he was not a visitor in their home. Miriam was always busy. Fasseke recalled the pain he suffered when he was introduced to her dates as a friend from Africa. Jake saw, surely he did, and tried to guide him away from his sister, who plainly, Fasseke saw, not only did not like him but despised Africa as well. Jake was patronizing in his own manner. He soon would be a gentleman and an officer in the army of the United States. He had no doubt that he would be sent to Korea, which was precisely where he wished to go to fight the Communists.

There was that date with Miriam, the one she squeezed in, the only, the last date, when he sought to tell her how, even after all these years, he loved her and thought she loved him too. Gently, she had removed his arms from around her waist. "Why, Chuma, that was a long time ago. In Africa. When we were children, I can't even visualize all that now. I'm an American, completely. I want American men and American money, and I expect to have had plenty before you finish Syracuse." She'd offered a pout. "Poor Chuma." She kissed him quickly on the side of his lips. "You'll find someone else."

But he had returned, even when Jake had gone into the army, hoping that something would change in Miriam. Nothing had. Fasseke would spend his brief visits with Reverend and Mrs. Henry talking about Pandemi and his family. The apartment would resound with Miriam's absence. (Even now he thought of the way she walked in New York, like a Pandemi woman with a bundle on her head, striding, bust thrust forward, buttocks well back, neck and head straight, as she'd learned when a child in N'Duli. It was no wonder men looked at her; the beauty of her motions carried to her face and body.)

Fasseke arrived in New York when Jake was on furlough. He was going to Korea when it ended.

"Let's dribble downtown and catch some bop, Chuma," he said. Fasseke suspected that would be better than trying to cheer him up; perhaps Jake had been tired of trying to cheer Fasseke up. Miriam was away. Fasseke tried to talk about her; Jake kept changing the subject. Finally, Fasseke said, "*Bo kende, Jake, bo kende.*"

Jake's face had knotted with trying to remember what the words meant. Fasseke, instantly regretting that he'd exposed himself so completely, hoped Jake would be unable to remember.

"I've forgotten what it means," he said. "What?"

Fasseke had forced a laugh. "What's dribble?" Then Jake laughed.

"It means to walk, to go, split, okay?" Jake said. "Now, what does *bo kende* mean?"

Fasseke had gestured admiringly to the city around them. He said, "It means 'this is all so nice.'"

"Oh," Jake said.

Fasseke never told him that the words really meant "help me."

The mood of pain and nostalgia passed. He was no longer the African bumpkin Jake may have thought he was; he was president of the country in which Jake had spent the first decade of his life. Jake was now a guest, to put it politely. Did he now understand the way of the world, that save for India and China, no colored nation possessed that essence of power symbolized by the ability and the will to produce nuclear weapons? Had he by now learned that wherever colored nations had gone in days of ancient triumphs, they merged with but did not dominate lesser cultures? Even the Chinese, with their gunpowder and compass. Could Jake have by now read that opening, one-sentence paragraph of the Richard Wright Lectures? Probably not. Poor Jake. Poor Richard. Both products of "white, Western Christian civilization."

Fasseke sighed when he heard the knock on the door.

Fasseke at first tried to fix Jake with an official though mildly warm gaze. But he found himself grinning broadly, like a boy who'd done well in spite of assurances that he never would, when Jake entered.

Jake entered the sun-swamped room, blinking, his eyes first picking up the blindingly clear blue sky and then the bluer ocean beneath it, both awash in sunlight, before he made out Fasseke's silhouetted form. Fasseke was advancing, shedding the light, it seemed, his arms held aloft from his sides, his teeth a glitter of white. Jake snapped to attention and saluted. "Mr.—" he began, but Fasseke was upon him, and Jake felt the stiffness flee from his own body as he, too, embraced.

"Jake."

"Chuma. I mean—"

They stepped apart and scrutinized each other through smiles. Jake said, "I've never hugged a president before."

"Nor I a major," Fasseke responded. "Jake, you look well."

He does, Fasseke thought, look well. Lean as a panther and eyes just as sharp. The bone structure of his face gives him that look, and his hair, cut close; no great, resounding Afro for Jake. "Come, let's sit down." Fasseke led him to the balcony. "We can get more air and a look at the scenery." Fasseke pointed to the north. "N'Duli's that way. We knew nothing about Bagui, did we, back then?"

"No, sir," Jake said. Why's it so hard to call the guy by his *name?* Jake wondered as he sat.

Fasseke eyed him, shook his head, and poured glasses of lime juice for them. "Listen, Jake. Be decent enough to call me as you know me." He smiled. "After all, I fixed it so you didn't have to go through the foreign minister, Mr. Kataka, who doesn't approve of every diplomat who's sent to Pandemi. Your paperwork for his portfolio is as good as done. A little pull, you see. So, in return you call me, please, Chuma."

Jake grinned again. "It's good to see you, Chuma." Surprisingly good, Jake thought. He *looks* like a president. But—and here he accepted the glass Fasseke held out to him. But, why is it so hard for me to *think* of him as a president?

"How are Reverend and Mrs. Henry?" Fasseke asked.

"In good health, but slowing down. They send their love to you—saw them before I left to tell them about this assignment—and to your family. How are they?"

"Mother died years ago, you know. Father lives here in Bagui, now, but refuses to live with us. My wife and me. He's about the same, but I believe he's slowing down too. My uncle Bonaco has a bus company. Actually, a single bus. Still very active, but then, he's a bit younger. And your sister?"

Jake said, "Working on her third divorce, my folks said. Lives in California now. We're not in touch as much as we once were."

"Pity," Fasseke said, "on all three counts. You have children, Jake? We knew from our parents when we were still corresponding that you'd married."

"Three. My family's in the States now."

"Oh, they should've come with you to see where you were born, Jake."

"My wife, Valerie, felt that after spending so much time in Europe, it'd be good for the kids to be back home for a while." The phrase "back home" lingered. Jake tried to rush over it.

"How about you, you have kids, Chuma?"

"No. I married a schoolmistress from Sierra Leone. She was at Fourah Bay College. We don't have children. Miriam?"

"No, Chuma. She never wanted any."

"I want them," Fasseke said, "and as far as we know, Yema and I *can* have them. The doctors agree on that." He looked out at the horizon. "Doesn't seem right, does it, an African without children? Both according to our tradition and in the West, where we're considered ungodly breeders. Consider yourself fortunate, Jake, and supremely blessed."

"Chuma, I try. I really try," Jake said, and they both laughed, and then gazed down at the city.

"Are you all settled, Jake?"

"Yes. They've got me set up."

"Aside from your duties—you've seen General Obika—?
Jake nodded.

105

"What're your plans? You've got to have dinner with us."

"Just let me know," Jake said. "But this afternoon I'm going to N'Duli to look around. Then there'll be all kinds of meetings and briefings at the embassy. General Obika'll take me on a tour of a couple of bases, and then I'll field whatever else comes my way."

"Jake, let me be frank with you. As I would be with a brother or good friend. We have no desire to become a part of an African NATO arrangement. One, we don't have the money to spend on defense, and anyway, against who or what? Two, if we did, we'd automatically belong to the American camp, the West. Now, you know as well as I do what's going on right now in the States. So we have enormous reservations about U.S. sincerity in its frequently cited concern for us, since it has never been demonstrated. For every bullet you give us, you'd want some kind of payment: bases, seaports, something. We're spread thin, Jake. We want to be in the world, not just outside it; our friendships have to remain true to every country that offers theirs in return and does not, in the end, hurt us. Third, I know Ambassador Fullerton requested that no military attaché succeed Captain Gilchrist. Jake, I know that."

Jake started to protest that he was not, realistically speaking, a diplomat, and that such observations properly should be discussed with Ambassador Fullerton. Instead, he extended his arms in a gesture of helplessness, and his eyes rode up to meet Fasseke's.

"Pandemi," he said, "is not a hardship post. I think I'm here to create the image that the U.S. and Pandemi are close friends. I've seen nothing that would warrant my being here except that and the fact that I know you. And I'm trying to finish out twenty years." Jake knew he had to throw it out. After all, Chuma had just said, in effect, *We know why you're here.* "I don't know what your intelligence says," Jake said, "but Obika put his finger on why I'm here, and that's to make the U.S. look pretty good with all of Africa because of what's going on back there. And I'm one of the pawns. I'm one of the pawns, Chuma."

"They think," Fasseke said, "we're all pawns, so we must make certain that none of us is, Jake. None of us." Fasseke finished just as a buzzer sounded for the next appointment. "My father is visiting N'Duli right now, Jake. You'll probably see him there. He'll want to talk to you. In the meantime, let's plan dinner for next week, shall we? I'm sure that whatever they have scheduled for you at the embassy, they'll let you come." Fasseke smiled as he stood and opened his arms. Without breaking his embrace with Fasseke, Jake sensed, quite suddenly, that someone was watching them. Jake was angered that he didn't know how long the person had been there. Bodyguard? Did they think *he* would make an attempt on Chuma's life? Klein, it appeared, wasn't as slick as he thought he was. But Fasseke was guiding him toward the door now, and the meeting was over, and that's what it'd been, a meeting, not a reunion. Down the stairs Jake walked, heat building at every step. He wondered how much Chuma knew and just how he'd come by whatever information he had. How much and how come. Should've backed off this one, Jake thought. There were two things he knew he'd have to do. The first was to stop thinking like Klein, stop thinking the way he had in Europe. The next was to start thinking, if he could remember how, like a black person. Especially *here*.

SEVEN

Coates had not been happy when Jake dropped him off at the embassy motor pool. Dawson had not been happy either, after shopping half the morning and cooking the other half.

But now Iris was beside him and they were, as far as he could calculate from the maps, already halfway to N'Duli. That made Jake smile. They had been so close to the big city and yet so far. The big city, yeah. Three streetlights then, maybe, and one store that sold Coca-Cola; a hotel filled with flying roaches and a gerrymandered house that they called a palace.

Jake glanced at Iris. Great-looking woman. He curled his eyes back to the road. This was his first time out of touch here. He'd not told Klein of this journey, and of course, Dawson had no business knowing anything. Jake took a deep, cool breath of Iris's perfume. Smells as good as she looks, he thought.

Iris too was pleased to be away. She'd left Ebu and Tuzyline gaping at each other when she swung out of the suite without warning when Jake knocked at the door. There'd been no word from Taiwo, nothing from Manoah. She'd not called the airline. If she was going to see anything of Africa, it'd be today.

"Red dirt," she murmured.

"What?"

"Red dirt. Didn't you notice it when you were growing up here? My mother came from the south. Mississippi. She often spoke of red dirt."

Jake's smile was quizzical.

"Take Spain," Iris went on. "Red dirt in the south, Andalusia, and yet there's that soft, white rock, like the cliffs of Dover."

"I didn't know you were into dirt," Jake said.

"What, do you think singers sing all the time?"

"No, I guess not. Know what they call singers here?"

"What?"

"The drummers."

"I've heard that," Iris said. "Like singers, each drum has a certain range."

"Right." Then Jake said, "Pretty, isn't it?"

"Yeah, it is. But I'm glad the car's air-conditioned because it's also pretty hot out there."

The car seemed to smooth out the bumps in the dirt road. Like a slow-moving rocket, red dust billowed lazily back behind them.

"What kind of music were they playing when you were home, Jake?"

Jake thought, then said, "I don't really know and didn't

have time to let it sink in, to tell you the truth. An awful lot of white rock groups—the Beatles, the Rolling Stones, Led Zeppelin—"

Iris interrupted. "What about Roberta Flack, Diana Ross and the Supremes, Aretha Franklin? What's happened to B. B. King, Bo Diddley?

Jake shrugged. "My kids tell me they're on the case, getting into new stuff as soon's the whites cop the old."

Iris laughed. "Well, knock on wood. I guess I'm still a novelty—or Europeans can recognize the real stuff—"

"You're great!" Jake said.

"Thank you, sir. But Ray Charles and the Raelettes do boss business in Europe, and Little Richard—forget it. They love the guy the way you got to love the guy that started all this boom, bang, and *zam* stuff, the costumes, the dances. Hey, they make it great for me; I'm a *coool* change of pace." She clapped her hands once with a resounding smack and barked out another laugh.

"Big star like you," Jake said. "Out here by your*self*. Like plain folk. How does that happen?"

Iris thought *hmmmmmm*, broke off the trails of her laughter and tartly said, "Because I wanted it to."

After a moment's silence Jake said, "Don't give me a wrong name, now. I'm *glad* you're here. Not only am I glad, I'm honored. He ignored the roll of her eyes. "It's not too cool going back to the womb alone."

Iris snapped her shoulders up. "That's just how you left it."

Oooo! Jake thought. He grinned and said, "Woweeeee!"

Iris found herself laughing. Yes, she had scored, caught him right in the chops, talkin' about some *womb*. But the guy had bounce, found his way back. "How were all those meetings this morning?" It looked like a long ride there and a long ride back. Be sociable, she told herself.

"Okay," he said, accepting the way out. "One was with President Fasseke."

Jake felt the atmosphere in the car change.

"Really?" Iris was leaning forward to more surely study his face.

"Yeah. We were running buddies when we were kids in N'Duli."

"Isn't that something." Iris leaned back in her seat.

Jake said, "He went to school in the States. Used to visit us. Liked my sister." He paused. "She didn't like him."

"Aw, too bad."

"No, good for him. Anyway, Chuma"—he glanced at Iris—"President Fasseke's father's at the village now. He went to my father's church. He was a village elder, you know, like a member of the town council. An ironsmith. Blacksmith, I guess they called them in the States."

"Ironsmiths made enough money to send children abroad?" Iris asked.

"No. They made a bunch of money on rubber during the war."

Iris gazed ahead down the long red road that was cut through the billowing green forests. They'd passed people along the roadside who'd waved at them, and she'd seen small clusters of thatched-roof homes. What, she wondered, did people *do* out here in the jungle. They swept by a sturdy woman striding down the road with a bundle of wood on her head. What had she to look forward to, Iris wondered, or her daughters, or her daughters' daughters? Could people like Taiwo and Fasseke make a difference? *Would* they make a difference?

"What'd you think of Ouro's plan?" Jake asked.

Iris was momentarily startled by the relationship of the question to her own thoughts.

"I don't know, Jake. I guess it's good if you're young, have a skill or trade, and you're mad about what's going on back home—the killings, the cops, cranking out new laws that they'll crank right back in when things cool down—"

"The young don't have skills or trades," Jake said briskly, "unless they're geniuses, and they see to it that, even when we produce them, they're not recognized as such."

"All right," Iris challenged, "what do *you* think?"

Jake grunted. "Some of these countries've tried to recruit Negro soldiers whose terms are up."

"And?"

"Zip."

"Really?"

"Zip. So they get all these crazy white boys, mercenaries. The black kids want to go back to what they know. Big buildings. The Cleveland Browns. Bars, churches. Sidewalks. Miniskirts, perfume—"

"What they call civilization."

"It's all they know. Africa is not on the agenda, but it seems to me that Pandemi is the very first country to even try to recruit Negroes. Seems a necessary first step to me."

"I wonder if the ambassador'll ask my brother."

"What's he do? What can he contribute?"

"He writes plays. Sometimes teaches."

Jake said, "Honest? Been on Broadway?" His tone was mocking.

"Yes," Iris said sweetly. "He's had three plays on Broadway and several off."

Jake saw two men emerge from the forest. They waved. Jake nodded. "What's your brother's name?"

"Joplin, too," Iris said. "Actually, Ralph Joplin, Jr."

Jake shook his head. "I don't know his work."

Iris smiled. The man was a diplomat sure enough. Usually people said, "Never heard of him," which was a rude and brusque consignment to oblivion. Not Jake. Jake was cool. She said, this time more sweetly than before, "I didn't think you had."

In the silence that followed, punctuated only by the hiss of cold air and the soft rumbling of the car, Iris pondered what kind of new music was likely to come out of a place like this. She'd heard Makeba, had caught the Ballet Africaine, had heard the chants and the choruses that sounded so much like church singing in her childhood, when her father sang in the choir. When she listened to records in Paris they brought back memories of sweating choir members, the slow, deliberate motion of fans bearing ads of the funeral homes, back and forth, forth and back. She sighed, momentarily weighted with memory.

She had heard in Europe, to her distress, that there was a Nigerian Miles Davis, a Senegalese John Coltrane, a Dahomean Dinah Washington. Sad, she thought, but at least they were imitating us for a change.

Iris thought of singers whose songs might do justice to a continent like Africa with all its differences in folk and

region. Aretha, certainly; *most* certainly. And, oh, yes, Miss
Sassie, Sarah Vaughn, and that British chick, Cleo Laine. Iris
frowned, trying to think of the singer from South America
whose voice was like one of the gorgeous birds she'd seen
flitting about. . . . Sumac. Yma Sumac? These, she thought,
could stand on the peak of Kilimanjaro, whose symmetry
was as graceful (she'd heard), particularly at dusk, as a Billy
Eckstine or Frank Sinatra ballad, and sing the whole continent to heaven. She envied them, Aretha, Sassie, Laine,
Sumac. Oh, she could bring down a cabaret, a small room,
maybe like Bobby. Intimate, they called her voice. Well, all
right; it earned a better than average living and, in Europe if
not at home, some reputation that drew even guys like Jake
Henry to hear her.

"He's a nice man, my brother," Iris said to break the
silence. "He could do long-distance things for this place."

"Yeah," Jake said. He was glad the silence had ended.
"Like what?"

"Teach down systems. Create new kinds of people. Just
with the facts that most others don't bother to teach."

"He one of those revolutionary Negroes?" Jake grinned at
her when he asked.

"If you think the truth is revolutionary, I guess so."

"Are you like him?"

Iris turned slightly in her seat. "I like to deal in truth. For
example, you hope that if not on this trip, if not somewhere
else, we'll get in bed, right?" She didn't wait for him to
answer. "Well, that's all right. Maybe we will. I've been to
bed with worse-looking men, men who don't let you see their
arrogance until afterward, like boys." She glanced out at a
trail that led into another cluster of huts and women beating

something in a big bowl with a very long stick. "I'm sort of lost here too," she said. "You kind of mentioned it. But, it's like you doing the womb alone, and it's all right, you know, to talk like that to someone, but I really hate bullshit. I really hate it, Jake. My business is ten percent talent and ninety percent bullshit. So is yours. So is very nearly everyone else's, so why should I get into a lot of fun and games? Guys like you run around grinning and carrying on, but you really should understand that bedding down is a fifty-fifty proposition, not one hundred percent talkin' trash and bein' cool."

Iris put her hand on his neck. She meant for the touch to be both soft and firm. "I wouldn't even be here if I didn't want to lay you. Just keep driving. I'll let you know when."

Jake grunted and something inside him, he didn't know what, seemed finally to let go of itself and he saw it falling like a thing with wings, looping, diving down to swoop upward again, tilting on a wing like a hawk in a warm wind; it was falling but never landed. It just kept falling.

The worn sign dangling from a tree said N'DULI and Jake turned off the main road. He had thought something about the region would be familiar, but nothing was. The road was so narrow that the people they saw walking along it had to spring aside into the tall grasses that lashed and snapped at the car as it rocked down into a cleared area graced by arching palms. Some of the houses that were set back among other trees had thatched palm roofs, others corrugated tin, brown with rust.

Jake seemed now to recall the last day when visitors came from other villages, walking in family clots, and dressed in brilliant holiday colors. The odor of roasting goat filled the air then, together with the raw, stinging smell of freshly uncorked palm wine. And from somewhere in the forest the drumming began.

But now it was quiet, as if all sound had been absorbed by great waves of climbing vines that embraced the trunks of huge trees. He recalled the quisqualis, with its heart-shaped blossoms, and the bonanox, which with the coming of night, would open their silver-white petals. People gazed at them. Some scowled with incomprehension; others smiled and waved or patted the car as Jake pulled behind a crimson, lime, and gold-painted wagon and parked. He stared around, past the gathering folk. Now the *feeling* of the place was familiar. And then he saw what remained of his father's church.

Iris turned at the sound of the sigh. She waited. It was *his* going back.

Jake turned off the ignition. "Ready for a walk around?"

"If you are," Iris said.

"Hello, hello," Jake said to the people when he got out.

"A-merican," one said.

"Negro," someone said.

"Niggero," someone else said.

Jake held out his hand to Iris as she came around the front of the car. Jake saw the men's eyes roll up and down her body, linger on her backside. The women suddenly stilled and commenced an intense scrutiny of Iris, whose smile danced beneath the oversized sunglasses she was wearing. She settled her wide straw hat more firmly on her head and took an extended hand and gave it a little pump. "Hello, there. Good to see you. Yes, we're Americans. Negroes. Negroes." The crowd seemed to fall back before her.

116

"That's the church?" Jake asked, searching faces for an affirmative response.

An older man who hung at the back of the crowd said, "Church? Yes, that's the church—" He broke off and bulled his way through until he was close to Jake. His head shot forward as fast and as straight as a snake's. "You the boy!" He cried. "Jacob!" He spoke rapidly to the crowd. A collective sound of wonder rose softly. Jake studied the man. The man jabbed himself. "I am called Brother Zinnah by your father, Reverend Henry." The man spoke to the crowd again. The people looked with new interest at Jake and Iris. Jake smiled and held out his hand. They shook vigorously, the man looking from Jake to Iris and back again.

Jake said, "This is my friend, Miss Joplin."

Brother Zinnah looked puzzled, but he inclined his head in Iris's direction. He spoke to the people again; they gazed once more at Iris.

"We just want to look around," Jake said. "And then see Mr. Fasseke. He's here, Brother Zinnah?"

"Akenzua is here, yes. I'll go tell him." He gave Jake and Iris a gentle shove. "Go, look about. N'Duli's not changed." He spoke softly to the people and they melted away, then returned to watch from a distance.

Jake led Iris to the church. Three concrete walls and less than half the roof remained. Before stepping inside, Jake turned to look at the wagon. It was the one he'd seen in Bagui.

"What?" Iris asked.

"I saw that bus in town the day after I got here. I think it belongs to Mr. Fasseke's brother."

"You didn't remember that man back there, did you?"

"No. He's got to be older than he looks."

"Good black don't crack," Iris said.

They entered through a doorway that had no door and stood on the threshold. They looked at the sky and the curving top of a palm tree whose leaves seemed to be protecting the hole in the ceiling. On the church floor was a clutter of browned palm leaves.

"Ten years," Iris heard Jake mutter. "Ten fucking years."

"Why did your family stay so long? Did missionaries do that?" She wished he wouldn't curse in church, even if it was falling down.

The rest of the roof would be coming down soon, Jake observed. He said, "They told my father—the church conference people—that if he did a double hitch, when it was up he'd get a good church and fall right in line for bishop."

Iris noticed that he was whispering, almost, just as she had. A soft wind swirled down through the opening in the roof and it brought momentary relief from the smothering heat. "And?"

Jake glanced at her as he guided her out. "They gave him the place in Amsterdam. Had about two people in the congregation. The church looked like this one. The parish was worse. We were hungry. And cold. So my father joined the army as a chaplain and we lived off his allotment." Jake thought he remembered the path to the big field where the goats were kept. He started in that direction, still holding Iris's hand. The people trailed them at a distance. "My mother taught Bible school and regular school."

"She must've been quite a lady," Iris said.

"I guess she was. I guess so."

118

"And your father a tough enough gentleman."

"He was a gentle man, all right," Jake said. "I never thought of him as being tough."

Iris teased him. "Not as tough as you, huh?" She laughed at the sharpness of his glance. "What're those flowers that look like hearts? Amazing."

"Quisqualis." And now he remembered: You crossed the field, keeping to the left of that great tree with the deep furrows in the bottom of its trunk that led down to roots, and behind it the path took you down an angled bank to a slow-moving brown stream where you swam and fished and sneaked through the grass to watch the girls bathe. There was a bridge made of logs and vines that you crossed to enter the deep forest, where you sat around fires at night and listened to stories about Ya and Ye and their son, Abi, and his son, Za, who married the cat woman, the peacemaker, and who bore Za Sera and Zuakpwa, twins; and around the fires he also heard of the Unknown Woman to whom one kind man gave elephant meat while the others jeered at her. She was a Magic Woman and made the kind man chief of the country. He heard the story of the singing waters, the petrified village and villagers who'd been turned to stone because of some evil deed done in the deep forest. . . .

"Jake! Hey! Slow down!"

They had crossed the field with the goats and the rank goat smell, and the trail to the stream lay ahead. They were perspiring and just starting to breathe heavily.

"Oh, hell," Jake said. "I'm sorry." He stopped so quickly that he braised the earth with his feet, his shoes sending red dust scooting around them. The people were on the other

119

side of the field, slowly walking in their direction. "This is the way to the deep forest," Jake said. "I suddenly remembered the way."

"Hummm," Iris said. "What's in the deep forest?"

"We're not going there. Just to the stream. It's not far. Down there." Jake pointed.

Shit, Iris thought. "Well, let's go." She was glad she'd worn sandals and pants, a thin blouse and the hat. She gripped his hand more tightly as they went down the path that was shaded by the trees. God, please, she thought. No snakes, okay?

It was several degrees cooler passing down to the stream. It was smaller than he remembered. He looked downstream and saw the bridge that led into the deep forest. The bridge seemed to cross more brush than water.

Iris kept her eyes to the ground, but sometimes she peered intently at the thick vines on the trees; the vines seemed to have just stopped moving when she looked at them.

"Spent every day after school here," Jake said. "Not Sundays, though."

"No, certainly not," Iris said.

Jake could no longer recall how many boys he slipped up on from behind and pushed screaming into the water or how many races he'd won swimming from one side to the other and back again. Chuma, Jake recalled, was not a good swimmer, and when the stream was running high never went in.

"Look the same?"

"Drying up," Jake said. He wondered how much longer it would be before dust replaced the brown water. The bridge wouldn't be needed then. The deep forest would be entered without ceremony.

"Someone's calling," Iris said hopefully.

They turned to the sound of voices and rapid footfalls. A band of boys shouting over one another called out, "Mr. Jacob, Brother Zinnah say come back! Mr. Fasseke want see you."

They'd walked briskly back to the car and Jake had shouldered the cooler. In the wake of the band of boys and the regal older folk, they'd wound their way through the village (Iris whispering: "Where did you live?" and Jake answering: "In a house next to the church. It's no longer there.") along the paths worn to a red-brown marble finish, paths that circled baked mud-and-straw houses, ran down in front of them, angled away from them, always with the sound of voices, an occasional shouting out (a question) and a shouting back (the answer).

"Can you understand them?" Iris asked. She had hooked one hand into Jake's belt to keep up. "What are they saying?"

"Not really. The child returns, something like that."

Now drumming started nearby.

Jake saw Brother Zinnah standing, beckoning beside a man who looked familiar. The crowd fell back with a murmur, and Jake saw behind Brother Zinnah and the man who looked familiar, the big house in which the village elders had met. It was bigger than the other buildings, and the path leading to it was smooth and hard. Jake slowed, the better to focus on the man next to Brother Zinnah.

"Jacob!"

Jake hesitated. He was not sure of the tone. In it he heard challenge, regret, relief. There did not seem to be any joy in it.

"Mr. Fasseke," Jake said, bending to lower the cooler and

rising to embrace the old man. His arms folded easily around the man, but the feel of him was like holding a bunch of wires that had not yet lost their sheathing, their insulation. They parted and studied each other. Behind him, not quite out of focus, Jake saw that everyone was smiling. He'd never seen so many smiles at one time. He found himself smiling, and when he glanced at Iris, *she* was smiling.

But Mr. Fasseke was speaking. "Jacob, so you have returned." He turned to the people. "The child returns home. The child returns home." He embraced Jake again.

"This is my friend," Jake said, for he sensed that Mr. Fasseke was gazing at Iris. "Iris Joplin."

"Your friend, not your wife?" Akenzua said. "Where is your wife? You have a wife?"

"Yes, and children," Jake said, smiling once again. "Miss Joplin is a friend."

"Welcome to N'Duli and Pandemi, miss," Akenzua said.

"Thank you," Iris said. "I'm happy to meet you all."

"True?" Akenzua asked. "What *young* woman is happy to meet an *old* man?" He laughed. "Come. Let's sit inside, where it's cooler. Jacob. Do you remember Bonaco. You used to call him 'Uncle,' like Chuma."

Jake shook hands. No wonder Mr. Fasseke looked familiar; Jake had seen him in the wagon the other morning. Inside, where it was indeed cooler, a breeze playing through the open spaces, Jake said, "Chuma told me you were here."

Akenzua's mouth fell open. He snapped it shut. Bonaco already was acting like someone was holding his feet to the fire. "Oh. He did? How . . ." Akenzua smiled more to himself than to anyone else. "I didn't tell him I was coming here. After a while, the children think they are your parents."

122

Akenzua shrugged. "But he's the president and of course knows all." Akenzua now tilted his smile at Jake.

Jake watched as the cooler was brought in and placed on the floor. Iris took off her sunglasses to wipe sweat from the bridge of her nose and then replaced them, slowly, and with a soft flourish, as though she'd wanted everyone who was in the structure to have at least one good look at her.

"How is your father?" Akenzua asked.

"He is well," Jake answered.

"And your mother?"

"She, too, is well," Jake said.

"And your wife?"

"Back in the States, and doing well. I was sorry to learn about Mrs. Fasseke," Jake said.

"Ah, well," Akenzua said. "And how many children do you have, Jacob?"

"Three, sir. Two boys and a girl."

"Good, good," Akenzua said, suddenly resentful of Chuma, who had none. "And why, my son, have you returned to Pandemi after so long a time?"

"A soldier goes where he's sent," Mr. Fasseke. "I'm at the American Embassy."

"Ah-hah," Akenzua said. He slid his eyes toward his brother.

Jake had seen the glance, but he fixed his eyes to the floor as if he had not. "The thing about Pandemis," he had overheard his father telling his mother long ago in New York, as though in direct reference to something that had happened (Jake did not know what), "is that they do not dissemble. Maybe that's true of all Africans? Maybe they can't. Or won't, or never had to learn how to, the way we had. If

123

they're angry or frightened, they don't try to hide it; if they're lying, somehow they let you know they are; if you're getting the better of them in bargaining, they smile in appreciation; if they're trying to conceal something, they tip you off, oh, they'll tip you off somehow."

Akenzua was speaking to Brother Zinnah, whose gaze kept coming to rest on Jake like a father's upon a son. "Is there food? We have guests. Bring food and something to drink. Can you have that done for us?"

Before Brother Zinnah could answer, Jake dragged over the cooler and opened it. He was sure he didn't want leftover boiled goat and starchy rice. As if reading his mind, Iris had seized the tablecloth and briskly spread it over the battered table in the corner. Jake wondered how much food Dawson had packed.

"They should be our guests, Jake," Iris said. Her stomach didn't feel too good. Too much heat, too much haste.

"Please, Mr. Fasseke?" Jake said, gesturing to the table. "Uncle Bonaco? Brother Zinnah?"

"And your sister, Miriam, Jacob," Akenzua said when they had demolished the chicken and crackers and cans of dessert and the wine. "How is she?"

"Oh, Miriam," Jake said. He watched Iris nibbling at a piece of chicken which she'd never finish, he thought. "She's all right, Mr. Fasseke."

"Married, too, and with children?"

"Third marriage, no children, sir."

Akenzua accepted a cup of the local beer and waited until Jake had one too. "Three times married? No children?"

"Yes. No."

Akenzua swallowed and swallowed again. "Too bad," he said. He was thinking how good it was that she had not married Chuma; a woman who married so often, never stopping to have children, was not a woman any Pandemi man should marry.

"More power to her," Iris said.

"Huh! I don't understand," Akenzua said.

"Maybe she hasn't found the right husband until now, Mr. Fasseke."

Akenzua glanced from Jake to Iris, then from Iris to Jake and back again. "Are you married, miss?"

Iris smiled. "No, I'm not. And don't plan to be again either."

Akenzua understood the words, but they didn't make sense. "No," he said, "not ever?"

"Well, I can't imagine it."

Akenzua shook his head. Jake lifted his beer to drink and conceal the great smile that was forcing itself onto his face.

Akenzua said, "American women are a puzzle to me."

Iris decided to let that pass. Old people thought they had certain rights of speech. You could not argue with them. They were set in their ways. Anyhow, it was time to start back. She was tired and not well, and she thought she would need all her energies to tackle the arrangements for getting back to—she'd almost thought civilization—Europe.

Wrong, her brother had told her. *Wrong.*

All right, Iris thought. Somewhere *else.*

Jake, attuned to the deceptive rhythms of the distant drums, had thought to be back on the hard road at least by dusk, which was fast approaching, galloping in the silences between himself and Akenzua. The stretching shadows seemed to conceal more expressions on more faces. He was no longer sure that what was on Akenzua's face was what he thought it was. Beer's a bitch! he thought. When, finally, he had managed to insert his need to get back to Bagui, when he sensed acquiescence in Akenzua and Brother Zinnah, he rose from the table, grasping Iris by the hand. Akenzua rose, too, gratefully, it seemed to Jake, and guided them back to the car, where Jake embraced him and Brother Zinnah, and agreed to visit Akenzua in Bagui. Uncle Bonaco was not there, had *not* been there for the past hour, Jake recalled. "And Uncle Bonaco? Where is Uncle Bonaco?"

"Perhaps asleep," Akenzua said in a voice that seemed as smooth as wind.

"I hope to see him again," Jake said.

"Most times he is at the market," Akenzua said. "Good-bye, Jacob. Come to see me."

"Good-bye, Mr. Fasseke. I will."

"Good-bye, miss."

"Good-bye. Good to see you." Iris said.

As they bumped and rolled and bounced back to the main road, Jake glanced at Iris, who seemed huddled in her seat. Not sleeping, but quiet, alone behind her partition of silence. There goes that, for now, he thought. A bush rat sped across the road in a blur of gray, and a bit farther on a brown bump in the road suddenly changed shape and became a ropelike creature straightening and twisting to escape the oncoming car. Jake felt something give beneath them, softly, and he thought to himself, I'd sure hate to be walking out here, man. Damn.

"They didn't like you too much," Iris said.

Jake was glad it was dark and she could not see his face. He'd not had that impression. "Why do you say that?"

"I felt it. You didn't?"

"No."

Jake felt that he was arriving back in familiar territory when he gained the hard road. He grunted with relief and mashed down on the accelerator.

Iris's voice was very small and very cautious. "What are you really doing here?"

Jake knew it was a question Akenzua had wanted to ask all afternoon, and maybe still would.

He watched the high beams knife down the road. He felt secure with General Motors wrapped around him. He lit a cigarette and lowered the back window and the sounds and smells of the forest whipped deeper inside the car and stormed out again.

"The real question is, Iris, what are you doing here? Do you know where you are or who you're with?" He punched some ash from the cigarette into the ashtray with his finger. He felt Iris lowering her partition.

"What does that mean? I ask a question and you answer with two."

"You ought to go back to Europe."

"I am."

"Sooner than that," Jake said, and the engine whined, then groaned, coughed, bucked, and the car slowed; he patted the gas pedal with his foot and the car seemed to respond, but started to buck again. Jake pulled over, shifted into neutral, and mashed the accelerator again. The engine seemed to die, but then, with a great pop, a massive blue cloud rose from the exhaust, purple in the taillights, and the car seemed to be running all right again. Jake shifted and moved off. The bucking diminished. He heard Iris sigh. "Something in the gas line," he said.

"Yeah, like what?"

"Palm oil, coconut milk, piss, I don't know."

"Why?"

"Because they don't like me." He thought of Uncle Bonaco, how he'd not been there to say good-bye. Bastard. *What do they know? How do they know it?*

"Okay. Why not?"

"That's what you said."

"Jake. Who are you?"

"You wouldn't believe me if I told you."

"Try me."

"I'm a soldier."

"Bullshit. You're The Man."

Jake smiled in the darkness.

E I G H T

★ 🦅 ★

"Nmadi, I didn't want to involve you in this," Fasseke said. "However, my friend, you must keep your eyes and ears open once you get to Washington, and let us know about anyone who seems . . . overly eager to get to Pandemi. Trust your instincts."

Fasseke was tired and not a little peeved with Shaguri, whose appetites had led to this hurried predawn meeting in Fasseke's house.

"Yes, yes, of course," Ouro said. "I just didn't know, but all the same I did exercise some caution."

Fasseke patted his shoulder and signaled for more coffee.

"I can't imagine her working with the major. The meeting was quite by chance. . . . " Ouro's voice drifted. He smiled at the floor. "One can imagine this situation, write about it without really knowing, and here it is, delivered on a silver platter." He raised his eyes and gazed at each person present: the Temian Manoah Maguru, Abi Pendembou, General Obika, Chuma Fasseke, and a man called Dawson.

"She'll be unable to leave until we're sure," Pendembou said. "No seats available on any planes out for two days." He fixed his gaze on Maguru.

Maguru wondered if all this would have happened if there'd not been that coup attempt. "All right. But as far as we're concerned, there's nothing. Coincidence, the meeting. Coincidence, two Americans taking a trip to where one of them was born. Nothing more." He paused. "Naturally, President Shaguri is upset that his friend went on the trip."

"Naturally," Fasseke said.

"The timing of her visit to Africa is unfortunate," Pendembou said.

"Abi," Fasseke said reproachfully. He was glad, though, that Pendembou had voiced his own thoughts. He had hoped that Shaguri would be reluctant to mix business and pleasure at this time. But he was the partner with the money and the jet fighters—with their loyal pilots and crews—and one did not criticize such a partner quickly. Yet, Fasseke guessed, it was Shaguri's weakness that had invited the coup in the first place, though it had failed. Fasseke had received word that as it began, Shaguri was just bidding adieu to Miss Temian of 1965. Fasseke turned to Obika.

"All's well in the north, sir. We are in constant touch with the Blue Squadron and radar, and we've increased the number of ground troops."

"Not enough," Fasseke snapped. "Two old men managed to get close enough to see the plant."

"They were Pandemis, sir," Obika said, knowing that Fasseke was making reference to his father and uncle.

"The Americans aren't going to walk right up there, General. They'll use Pandemis the way they used Temians."

"That won't work at Jija Deep, sir," Obika said, unruffled. "We knew the two old men were your relatives."

"And what of down here, General, if they try to oust me?"

Obika said, "You're better protected than you know, sir. We see them going after the plant, not you, in any case. If the plant had been in Temian, they'd have gone after that to teach President Shaguri a lesson about the price of his oil. But the plant is here, so they went after him. Others would have learned the lesson."

Fasseke was pleased with Obika. He smiled. "This protection? What does it consist of?"

Pendembou said, "If we told you, you might tell your father and then the protection is compromised." He smiled across at Obika, who glanced at Fasseke.

Good God, Fasseke thought. He remembered the conversation with his father. Chagrined, he said, "The point's well taken."

"Sir?"

Fasseke turned to Dawson.

"I've got to get back, sir. To be the good servant the American embassy people want me to be."

Fasseke nodded. "Thanks."

The others touched his hand briefly and Dawson slipped out. Moments later they heard a small car hum off.

"Well, Abi," Fasseke said. "Let us all hear the morning briefing."

131

Pendembou raised no questions about the presence of Obika and Ouro and Maguru. As planned. To gain their confidence. Pendembou merely glanced around, his eyes questioning, and Fasseke nodded. Pendembou slipped his hand into his snakeskin bag and brought it back into view with a single sheet of paper. He said, "Ambassador Fullerton is said to have received word from friends on the Foreign Affairs Committees—House and Senate—about Jija Deep. We think he remains our friend."

"I see him this morning."

Pendembou continued. "Karpinskov will ask you this afternoon what the Soviets can do to help us maintain Pandemi sovereignty. I think they view Pandemi as a potential base. Not as close as Cuba, but not all that bad from the southeast."

Ouro said, "Missile base?"

Obika said, "Why not? Why wouldn't they think that? But the answer is no."

"A definite no," Fasseke said. "If necessary, we'll be our own launching pad. No one else's. And Hua-Ling, Abi?"

Pendembou's smile was stiff; it always was. "We think he's heard something but doesn't yet know what it means. He's late afternoon. He wanted this morning."

Obika patted his cheeks, as though he were patting down a beard. He tapped Ouro. "I don't know if you writers understand such things, but we have all this commotion, troops and planes on the alert, bits of information coming in from all over. The great powers assembling all around us. What has Pandemi done? Built a plant that provides power and also waste which we hope to use in the future, near or far. Does that say anything to you, Mr. Writer?"

"General," Fasseke said. He tried to keep the weariness from his voice. "It probably says more to him than we realize."

Ouro moved vigorously in his seat. "Can I speak, Mr. President? I heard a certain tone in the general's voice that I'd like to respond to."

"Nmadi."

"It says only what it must say, General, what it has always said, that the big powers feel they must maintain power. Once, of course, when generals were more thought of and more visible—in the European, not African sense—they took power through outright aggression, generals directing the charge. But the world tells itself its nations are now above such things and power is clothed, sheathed like a sword, covered like a gun out of use. Yet the use of power is everywhere obvious. That's all it says, General, but for all that, we recognize the beast for what it is as writers always have. . . ." Ouro sat back in his chair. He peered at Obika.

"You must read Ambassador Ouro, General," Pendembou said.

Obika grunted, but he smiled at Ouro. "I have."

Enough, Fasseke thought. He rose and said, "Gentlemen, thank you." He crossed the room and shook hands with Maguru, Obika, and Ouro and then, with Pendembou, left the room.

Maguru looked at his watch. "I have to get back," he said. "Forgive me if I don't linger." He shook with Ouro and Obika and swept out of the house.

"Ambassador," Obika said, "can I drop you off or do you have your car?"

Ouro concealed his surprise by pretending hesitation. "I keep forgetting the car," he said. "I suppose you never do. You've been a general far longer than I've been an ambassador."

Obika laughed. "I can't forget. Not in uniform, anyway. Whoever heard of a general walking?"

"But you're not in uniform now."

"True," Obika said. "I was sleeping when the call came, as you must've been. I grabbed the handiest clothes. Generals don't sleep in their uniforms."

"Well, then let's walk and talk, what do you say?"

Obika had never had a chance to talk with a famous writer. He was thinking of writing a book himself. "My driver?"

"Send him along."

"And yours, Ambassador?"

"He's probably given up reminding me that I'm supposed to ride. If he's there, I'll send him away too."

"You're on, Ambassador. It's been a long time since I walked, especially this early in the morning. Do writers do this often?"

"Most, I think, would rather ride," Ouro said.

Alone in a breezeway through which the rising sun slipped sharply, Fasseke said, "What, Abi?"

"Maguru seemed assured. In control. Unafraid. And our people assure me that the coup *was* crushed, and Shaguri will meet you tomorrow."

"Good, good."

"You look tired."

"I *am* tired."

"Yes, it's been a busy day, a busy night, a busy week."

"Not yet over, Abi. It's just beginning, the rest of our history."

"Ah, but we knew that, didn't we?"

Fasseke slipped Pendembou's gaze; his eyes framed an asking such as might be found in the eyes of a teammate reluctant to question your ability, your willingness, to finish the game. "Of course we knew," Fasseke said.

But he was tired, tired as with the weight of a panther upon a limb of his mind. Yes, they'd anticipated the reaction to Jija Deep. He had thought of that hundreds, thousands of times, and each time he'd responded crisply to the moves by the outsiders. Action. Reaction. Reaction. Reaction. You made the first move, they reacted and you reacted forever or until you were able to act once again and fear no reaction whatsoever.

How, Fasseke wondered, could a single man—president, prime minister—hold all the acts of all the people in place all the time, men who ruled nations one hundred times larger and more complex than his? They didn't because they couldn't. It was that gossamer thread of faith in a common destiny. Only *that* created states and maintained them, good or not. Still, one tried to delegate power to trustworthy subordinates who were extensions of that one man. But which were they? Who could tell until the morning of some ides of March or May, July, or October?

Shaguri had felt the winds, but survived, for now, and Fasseke himself had felt stealthy steps along the path to his cemetery when he first heard of the coup. Good Obika, he thought. But military men had led the uprising against Shaguri. Generals and colonels, formerly or presently, or men with minds like theirs, sat astride the globe. What will it be like when sergeants and privates take over, Fasseke wondered.

"I suppose you'll go right to work, Abi?"

"Well, yes, I'm up now, sir."

They walked to the courtyard, through it to the door.

"Listen," Fasseke said. "I take it from what Obika said that my wife also is under watch?

"Yes, naturally. And we ought to look after your father as well, to save him from himself." Pendembou laughed. "You're still very much alike, you know."

"Is that bad, Abi?" Fasseke laughed now.

"Not at all. Good night. See you in a few hours."

"Good night, Abi." Fasseke closed the door. Abi, he thought, can I trust you? And then as he left the courtyard for his bedroom, he said through tightly clenched teeth, "Oh, damn!"

Ambassador Fullerton awaited the arrival of his "cultural affairs officer." He needed this meeting before seeing Fasseke. Fullerton fumed. Perhaps the time was near (it was 1966, after all) when ambassadors would be nothing more than figureheads or rich old men who'd heavily bankrolled a president's campaign, tottering around to teas and cocktail parties and being interviewed by the press of the host countries where they were assigned. (Kennedy's press buddies wouldn't last long without Jack the Zipper around.) But, Fullerton thought, not now, at least, not here and above all not him. He meant to count for something, whether Averell approved or not. Whoever heard of such a title anyway, Secretary of State for African Affairs? Averell, who sometimes didn't even bother to get off the plane when it landed at some baking African airport. "Hello, Ken," he said when Kenneth Klein entered, guided in by the secretary.

"Morning, Mr. Ambassador," Klein said respectfully.

Fullerton did not ask Klein to sit. Neither did Fullerton stand. "Ken, I understand what President Fasseke has here is a fast breeder reactor. I want you to know that I thought as much. I now have confirmation. Power, yes, and plutonium, yes." Fullerton waited. He could afford to. His information came from friends on the House and Senate Foreign Affairs and Intelligence Committees. Youngsters like Klein believed you were as ignorant as *they* thought, and that you could survive American politics without connections, that you could arrive at any post without them. A very few did, but most did not.

Fullerton bullied his way into Klein's silence. "We could have worked on this together. We're supposed to be on the same side."

Klein did not answer. Fullerton was angered by the way he just stood there before him, not victor and not victim. A presence. A good German, Fullerton thought, and a better Nazi.

"Yes, sir," Klein said. Jake Henry's voice came to him; he sounded just then quite like him.

Fullerton recognized the empty response. "For station chief you don't have a lot to say, do you?"

Klein did not like this old man. He had old ideas. He couldn't take a post that never was what history said it was and pull some neat, nice costume over it.

"You're going to take the plant out. When? How?"

Klein remained silent. He had nothing to fear from Fullerton, and he knew Fullerton knew it.

"That's why Major Henry's here, to help." Fullerton waited.

Klein remained motionless.

"Sovereign territory doesn't mean anything anymore, unless it's ours, eh, Klein? Maybe we'll learn a lesson in Vietnam, as the French did. But here we're going to do what the Chinese haven't yet done to Tarpur, what the Soviets haven't yet done to Dimona?" Within, Fullerton snarled. Damn! To these people Manifest Destiny was endless; it meant moving farther westward until they'd overrun the world. Damn Luce and his goddamn 'American Century.'

"Sir, you know the Soviets are interested in Pandemi too."

"Only because we are, Ken, and that gives us reason to assign spy ships, rotting and rusting, like the *Belmont*, humping and pumping up and down the coast of this beleaguered continent from which every nation that today considers itself civilized—except Russia—created its wealth. According to you guys. This place over which every hour or two fly satellites whose direction and control of them Jack Kennedy abdicated to DOD, maybe because, like Shaguri, he was often distracted by other matters?" Fullerton marched from behind his desk and planted himself directly in front of Klein.

Klein looked up at him, at the fierce eyes and downplunging bushes of eyebrows. It was like looking at an eagle.

"Say something," Fullerton said. "Spy. Shithead." God, he hated these people.

Klein had backed up before this blast of sibilants and spit.

"You offered Onwonwu in Temian fifteen *million* dollars to kill Shaguri and he refused. So you went to a lieutenant and offered him fifty thousand to do the job. You see what happened. It happens wherever you people operate. You're pitiful," Fullerton said with scorn, "but yes, dangerous, because you've created another level of foreign policy. We don't know what you're doing, and you don't care what we're doing."

Fullerton turned and gathered up some papers from his desk. He thrust them toward Klein, together with a pen. "You're resigning from the Foreign Service."

Klein backed up. He smiled slowly, the way he would had he been facing a person who'd suddenly revealed his insanity. "Sir, I've never been *in* the Foreign Service."

"Thanks, Ken. That's all." Fullerton replaced the pen and papers on his desk.

Klein edged out of the room. The sonofabitch has cracked up, he thought. He can't be trusted. Gotta hurry up, get this thing going, because Fullerton loyalties were with a dream, not the hard stuff, not today.

Satellites my ass, Klein thought when he had entered his office and closed and locked the door. The packet of NPIC photos in the back of his file, the same photos he'd been looking at when summoned by Fullerton he remove, and one by one spread across his desk. *Triple* confirmation, Klein thought. Land, sea, and air. Fullerton's got friends . . . so *what*?

The phone rang and Klein picked it up. "Really? Honest? No shit?"

"I want to leave to*day*. They're telling me I can't. The airlines are saying they have no seats. I can't get an exit visa. What the hell's an exit visa? I have to get official permission to leave someplace?"

The second secretary and political affairs officer recoiled

before the power of Ms. Joplin's outburst. She was, he observed, worn and angry, probably from the ride to the airport, where they would not give her an exit visa, and back here to the embassy.

"Well, they sort of go together, Ms. Joplin. Bagui isn't like New York or Paris, where there're planes going and coming all day long. The airlines say they have seats, but for a specific day. Not just any day."

"Today. Today. This morning. Air Senegal reserved a seat for me direct to Paris."

"But they didn't give you the ticket because you had no exit visa, right?"

"Mr. Secretary, I wouldn't be here if you were wrong."

The second secretary said, "In places like these, Ms. Joplin, things sort of have to be coordinated. The visa, the ticket."

"Don't you understand? Without the ticket, they won't give me the visa and—"

"Without the visa, you can't get the ticket. I know. This is Pandemi. Africa. I suggest you check back into a hotel and take things one at a time. You should be able to get out tomorrow. In the meantime, I'll see what I can do, all right?"

Iris nodded, nodded but tried to keep the alarms that were going off in her head at a low volume. It was weird, this sense of entering a country as one entered most countries, assured through who knew what, that one could come and go with a minimum of bureaucratic mumbo-jumbo at customs, that one was both welcomed and respected as a traveler and treated with courtesy because the hosts did not know when they themselves might one day find themselves abroad and would want similar treatment. That code existed long before legal frames were set about it; they were, as most laws, at first moral.

Gone was Manoah Maguru; gone was Shaguri (or at least, she had not heard from him) and gone were Ebun and Tuzyline, like fast, scudding, dark clouds whipping off to the east. She had tried to reach Nmadi Ouro, who was "unavailable." How different it'd been when she entered! With the big car and Manoah growling orders, the place near the border with so many men and guns. And suddenly she was alone and did not know why.

"Call me as soon as you check in, so I'll have your number, will you? Don't worry. This happens all the time."

"Tell me—just where do I get this mysterious exit visa?"

"Oh," the second secretary said. "Either at the Home Ministry Offices in the Government Building or at the airport."

"Shit!"

"Beg your pardon?"

"Why didn't they tell me that while I was out there?"

"It might not have done you any good, Miss Joplin," the second secretary said softly, and in a voice that would have made her ask what it was he meant except she saw and recognized the stride, long, insinuating, even before she saw his color or his face. She rushed to the door and called at his back: "Jake!"

Jake stopped, turned, framed a smile. "Oh, hey. How goes it, Iris?" He returned to the door and peered in at the second secretary and political affairs officer. "Morning, sir." They had met only briefly, when Jake was leaving Klein's office and the second secretary was entering. But Iris was pushing him out into the hall. Jake gave way before the flurry of her hands.

"I have to talk to you, Jake."

"I thought you left."

"Yeah, me too. Something about papers. Exit visa."

"I told her we'd get on it," the second secretary said as he walked down the hall.

"Good," Jake said. They both watched him walk to the end and wheel around a corner. "Where are you staying?" He saw that she was both angry and frightened. In such cases fright rushed to the front. "The Ashmun?"

"I guess."

"C'mon. Ride you over. If you don't mind going with The Man."

Iris slid her eyes toward him while they got her luggage from the receptionist, an attractive young Pandemi woman. They are always attractive, Jake thought.

"But you're a black man," Iris said as he placed her luggage on the walk outside before going to get his car.

"So is Nmadi Ouro," he said. He left her waiting while he soothed Coates and brought the car around front under the gaze of the duty marines. In the car she sighed and lay her head back against the top of the seat.

"Yeah, and he's a friend of my brother," she said. The movement of the car reminded her that she'd been going and then coming back for half the day already, and was still here. "But you're a black American," she said.

Jake pulled out around a man pushing a gigantic hand wagon loaded with old tires. "Why don't you tell me what's going on, Iris?"

She laughed. "You already know, probably. I just want out.

I read in the paper that Taiwo Shaguri almost got kicked out of Temian."

"Almost killed," Jake said. "Do you know him?"

Iris hesitated. The bargaining session had started. She took a deep breath, confided with her instincts, and said, "I came down to be with him."

"Bad timing."

"Nobody told me. Tell me about it."

Jake hunched his shoulders. If Ouro couldn't help her, that meant they knew something was up and he had been so advised.

"He really couldn't help you, eh?"

"Who?"

"Ouro."

"I said I couldn't reach him."

"Last night he seemed eager to keep in touch. But that was last night, I guess. Can't Shaguri deal with someone over here?" He knew the answer to that too.

"I can't reach him either."

"Don't worry. We'll get you out."

"Is it going to be bad?"

"What?"

"Whatever's going on. Ulcuma's claiming the territory where Pandemi and Temian meet. Read that in the paper too. There was a map."

Klein's been busy, Jake thought. Jesus. "Yeah? Didn't read it today. What else?" Jake knew the drill. Klein covered all the bases."

"I didn't finish the story," Iris said. They were now at the desk of the Ashmun. "You want to come up?"

"Can't now. How about dinner?" He saw her face become

edged with disappointment. "You won't be able to get out for at least another day. He told you that at the embassy, didn't he?"

"Yes. Yes, he did. Okay. Can you spare the time, Major?"

Jake chuckled. "I surely can. The Man has all the time in the world. That's why he is The Man."

"Tell you, really, Jake. I don't give a damn if you're Satan. Just get me *out of* here!"

NINE

Throughout Karpinskov's meeting, Fasseke thought of the one earlier, with Fullerton.

The old man had been intense with his pledge of U.S. friendship and a level of aid that would surpass the combined levels of every black country on the continent, except, perhaps, Temian's. Temian, of course, had oil and most of the "aid" was in the form of trade.

Fasseke found the timing of Fullerton's pledge curious—though not really. He wanted something in return, or his country did, and the only thing Pandemi had now was Jija Deep. The U.S. had its own iron—which it was finding cheaper not to dig up, since it could get quality ore from abroad more cheaply. It didn't want the gold, because the reefs in South Africa seemed inexhaustible. It didn't want crops. It simply wanted Pandemi not to have what it had just built.

Fasseke inquired as to the U.S. position on Ulcuma's sudden territorial claim. "It's already under study," Fullerton had said, "but I don't see how we could properly intervene with a statement of support for Pandemi or Temian, not at the moment anyway, since my political affairs officers are still gathering background."

"Ah, yes," Fasseke had said, offering Fullerton more coffee, which he declined. "We thought, however, that by now there'd be some comment from your government on the events in Temian."

Fullerton had said, shaking his head, "Terrible, terrible. We will be making a statement, of course."

"That will be very interesting," Fasseke said, and looking at Fullerton, he had seen for the first time in two years an unhappiness, even, fleetingly, a shame, in the man's eyes. And there was in the tone of their talk the atmosphere that attends the delivery of unvoiced warning; it was all the more pronounced since not once did the ambassador mention Jija Deep.

Fasseke liked the man, but knew when he said good-bye that nothing between them would ever be the same. It was not unexpected, but he was sorry nevertheless. What could the man do? What was he to say? One simply could not be disloyal to one's country when he accepted such a position. They knew Fullerton better than he knew himself. Fasseke did hope, however, that the ambassador could quickly get back to his friends (perhaps Ouro should be sent off at once to contact them himself?) in time to build a preventative hue and cry.

Fast upon Fullerton's departure, Fasseke summoned Pendembou, who had said without coaxing, "They will try something." The meeting had been piped to Pendembou's office, where he had sat making notes.

Days earlier, even before the arrival of Jacob Henry, Fasseke, Pendembou, Obika, and Kataka had run through the scenarios:

The French: Even though pushed into the Pacific because they lost the Algerian War and could no longer test nuclear weapons in Algeria, and because they'd also been humiliated in Vietnam, the French wanted to maintain good relations with their former colonies in Africa—Senegal, Dahomey, Chad, etc., and with Temian and its oil. Also, they wished to neutralize U.S. influence. Former colonies still were economically viable trade regions as well as unending cheap labor pools for work within and without Metropolitan France. If at all involved in the destruction of Jija Deep, it would be for reasons that impinged on the totality of French well-being. At this time, forget the French, who are desperate to avoid any collusion with the U.S.

The Portuguese: Too busy in Angola and Mozambique. Signs of imminent revolution at home. Weakest NATO partner. Not even trusted as a surrogate.

The British: Very busy in South Africa, India, Nigeria, Kenya, Rhodesia, the Caribbean, etc. Trying to maintain a profitable level of trade in the face of growing U.S. multinational influence. Shell BP in Temian. Colonial mindset, however. Caution.

Soviets: Cannot offset old colonial influences. Increasing trade with Cuba makes difficult significant trade with African nations. Guinea an example. This region convenient for Soviets: warm water bases, "view on the West." African students report racism against them in Soviet Union. Particularly vicious. They're not immune. Indicates caution when dealing with Soviet diplomats. Caution. Caution. Weapons high priority trade item, but to accept provides overt excuse for coup attempt.

Chinese: Too many internal problems: cost of maintaining Amur River garrisons in the West and monitoring Japanese and Soviets in the East, and extensive border watches on their southern borders across Asia. Trade? Little, if any, value to us. Weapons okay, though not modern. Also acceptance invites possible coup attempt.

African nations: Ulcuma is the only nation, save perhaps Chad, with nothing. Pawn, not strong enough to be surrogate. Always attempting to further its border claims. Excellent point of departure for two-pronged attack on Pandemi and Temian, by mercenaries, of course. No problem foreseen with containment and destruction of such forces.

The U.S.: It knows of Jija Deep, but can only covertly intervene to cause its destruction. Must use a surrogate force or hire a domestic one. May use Ulcuma's border claims for its own advantage, regardless of wish not to alienate OAU and the rest of African Africa. Must maintain good relations with Temian. Knows of Shaguri's stated preference for closer ties with U.S. However, U.S. a constant interventionist in opposition to independence movements. Wishes their multinationals to control all trade. Diplomacy, covert actions are supportive. The main problem, without doubt. N.B.: U.S. covert actions are not always known or approved by the current administration until under way or complete. Viz.: Ambassador Fullerton.

"Is Kataka with you, Abi?"

"Yes, sir."

"Good. How soon would you think the Americans will start?"

"If you exclude what's happened in Temian, without luck, and what's now beginning in Ulcuma, which is pointless, within the next forty-eight hours."

"Get Nmadi off to Washington on the next plane, and have him talk to Fullerton's friends as soon as possible, if not sooner."

"Right away," he had said.

"Well, Mr. President," Vladimir Karpinskov was saying, "we're glad you have the new power plant. We'd like to help you modernize, if that's what you wish. I believe we've indicated that before. If you prepare some proposals—"

Here Karpinskov smiled and shrugged. He had suggested such proposals many times before. "—we will give them primary consideration."

"Mr. Ambassador, you must know how precarious our financial situation is at present," Fasseke said. It would take us quite some time to repay whatever you could help us with."

Karpinskov said, "I understand, sir, but between friendly nations such repayment can always be arranged."

Karpinskov's English was good, if markedly accented, and like so many Soviet diplomats Fasseke had met, he did not appear to have ever missed a meal in his life. "I know you're very busy right now, Mr. President. But one final thing: it's being said that the new plant is powered with nuclear fuel." Karpinskov waited.

"I'm sure you have already accepted the rumor as fact, Ambassador Karpinskov," Fasseke said.

"It's a fact then?" This time Karpinskov did not wait. "The

presence of such a plant here is—is a remarkable step forward, sir. Double congratulations! Perhaps in direct regard to this we can offer assistance?"

Fasseke said, "Undoubtedly we will require some assistance through certain departments of your government, Mr. Karpinskov. We would not like for such an African achievement to befall an accident of any kind, you see. They happen all the time, these accidents."

Karpinskov nodded. "I understand, Mr. President. I will talk to Moscow. But is there anything else we can do for this great nation?"

"That would be of tremendous help to us," Fasseke said. But he knew, as did Karpinskov, that should there be an accident, there was nothing they could do save point fingers, and since the magic that leaped forth from the pointed finger vanished millennia ago, the gesture would be useless.

Karpinskov, on his departure down into the heat, where he saw that more soldiers had come on duty, considered the complication, for that's what it was; a have-not nation seeking to obtain the ultimate weapon to defend itself through actual use or the fact of just possessing it. Nevertheless, it was a threat to stability and balance in the world. Fasseke would not rule forever, perhaps not even until fuel conversion took place. Who knew what his successor would be like? There were already enough such irritants: China, Israel, South Africa, India, and one would be a fool to discount the Japanese. Undoubtedly, at some time, Cuba, naturally, and that might prove to be another October 1962. But who could tell? Nothing ventured, nothing gained. It might be best, yes, quite possibly so, if the Americans arranged an accident.

He always seems so merry, Fasseke thought as he listened and watched Hua-Ling and found himself smiling too. The Chinese ambassador spoke vaguely and in halting English of the possibility of a trade agreement, the loan of mining experts to get at the iron and the gold. (But Fasseke knew he was more interested in the gold than in the iron ore because China had unlimited reserves of iron.)

"I have heard," Hua-Ling said, "that your plant is powered with nuclear fuel. Is true, Mr. President"

"Yes, Mr. Ambassador, it is true."

Hua-Ling nodded. He wondered just how they'd done it. The Chinese had had the bomb only two years. "It should be easy to get rid of spent fuel in a place as large as Africa."

"We don't have to worry about that just now," Fasseke said.

Hua-Ling was halfway through his third Coke. "Can we be of any assistance, Mr. President?" His smile widened and his eyes danced above plump cheeks.

Fasseke rested his lips against the tent of his fingers as though absorbed in deep thought. "It may be that you can help us at the moment, Mr. Ambassador. We are very careful with our new plant. We have experts there, but accidents do happen, you know. We don't want any accidents."

Hua-Ling smiled at his Coke. "Who would, sir? Who would want such a terrible thing to happen?" He paused. "But I see the point you are making. Agreed. We will do what we can, where we can, of course. One must always be on watch, for things often are not what they seem to be. And—ah, yes! I've been advised that the Ulcuma claim is groundless. Strange that it's been put forward again at this time, wouldn't you say so?"

"Absolutely, Mr. Ambassador."

"Then we will make a public assessment."

"Thank you; we're very grateful."

Now Fasseke sat in his office with Pendembou and Kataka.

They sat in silence, looking out at the sea, for it was time for the Green Flash. Silence seemed to make their vision keener as the top of the sun sped downward beneath the sea.

"There!" Kataka said, half-crouched above his chair, but Fasseke and Pendembou continued to search the horizon a second longer, as though their eyes might catch up with something missed.

"I saw nothing," Fasseke said.

Pendembou said almost cautiously, "I'm not sure what I saw—something? Nothing?"

It had happened before that people in the same group, watching at the same time, saw it while others did not. It was said to be better, in some mysterious way, if all saw it rather than some. Frequently, those who did not see the Green Flash lied and said they did so as not to cause wonder among those who truly had seen it.

The silence gathered a thickness.

Dusk began to enshroud the room, and the wind licked through in tentative gusts; the rainy season was due and the winds changed. Streetlights came on below. The jeeps that patrolled the grounds now beamed headlights.

Segbeh Kataka said, "Only Hua-Ling asked us to check the wording of his statement. Of course, Karpinskov's people never do that."

"The Soviets are arrogant about their poor command of English," Pendembou said. "If they say anything at all of value, it will be translated well by at least a half-dozen sources."

"The meeting with Shaguri," Fasseke said impatiently. "It's confirmed?" He knew he was being unduly annoyed that he hadn't seen the Green Flash, but he couldn't help it.

"At the Mountaintop, as planned," Pendembou said. "And something else: Obika's people report that small arms have arrived in Ulcuma, but he foresees no problems he can't handle."

Kataka looked up from his writing. "I think the press conference may push the Soviets along in our direction and even get some others to complain about the U.S. plans. Pity we don't have television yet." He pushed his heavy spectacles down the wide bridge of his nose and resumed writing.

"Armed intervention," Pendembou said, "in our domestic affairs, and in African affairs," he said to Kataka. "Put that in someplace."

The press conference would begin with an address by Fasseke. The need to make such an address had come far more quickly than he wanted. But he would nevertheless tell the Tribes today what America was doing and what Pandemi was doing about them; he would tell them what kind of plant was at Jija Deep, and why; tell them who was behind the failed coup in Temian, of American covert support to Ulcuma, a nation unloved by Pandemis. Ulcuma would become a pariah, even among the pariah states of Africa. Fasseke believed his talk would unite the Tribes; he hoped it would arouse world condemnation of the U.S. as well, though this he seriously doubted. There was, finally, nothing else to do now.

153

Since they began it, Fasseke thought, let it all be revealed now so that whatever happens does not happen in silence.

"Come," Fasseke said in response to the soft knock on the door.

"Ambassador Ouro, sir."

Nmadi Ouro entered, dressed in a dark suit, white shirt, and tie. He shook hands with Fasseke, Pendembou, and Kataka, who earlier in the day had briefed him on the duties of his new post.

"I'm ready, Mr. President. I'm packed and ready."

"But you have time to sit for a moment, Nmadi. Please."

Ouro found a chair and sat.

"Griffin is meeting you," Kataka said. "That's only just been arranged. You won't have time for any formalities, not now. We'll make the announcement of your appointment and departure at the press conference."

Ouro said, "Press conference?"

"Yes, Nmadi," Fasseke said. "In a couple of hours. The news people around here are more impressed when you call a conference at an unusual hour. And that pretender from Paris is in town, I hear, the Fearless Frenchman. Except he's an American. But things've become complicated even more, Nmadi. We need you, not Griffin, to talk to Fullerton's friends in Washington and to talk to your own friends. Abi says we've got no more than two days before things break on the border, probably in concert with whatever's going to happen at Jija Deep."

"We want as many people as possible to know what's going on and maybe that'll put pressure on the Americans. Maybe," Pendembou said.

"I understand," Ouro said.

"Griffin's preparing a press conference too, Nmadi," Fasseke said. "It'll serve the purpose of announcing a change in the post. We want to do it this way to underline that there's no break—apparently—in continuity. But you'll have the details of the situation here, which you will announce at once." Ouro accepted the packet Kataka was handing to him. "Before you announce them, however, warn Griffin. He may be surprised, but he'd better not show it."

Ouro fumbled with the packet. Fasseke stood and said, "Read that on the plane, Nmadi," he said. To Pendembou and Kataka he said, "Excuse us a moment," and he guided Ouro to the balcony, into the stiffening wind. He placed an arm around Ouro's shoulder.

"Nmadi, we need you now more than ever. You know now about the Americans and Ulcuma. We're not sure we can get even verbal support from the Soviets, and hardly anyone listens to the Chinese when they speak about Africa. Realistically, you know we can't expect much from the British or the French or the West Germans. Even if we could, the Americans would run over them. Listen, Nmadi. Nothing, *nothing* has changed since we were boys in London. *We* are on the verge of change; *they* want us as we were. As you told Obika, they've responded as they always have. Maybe no one cares what happens to us. I don't completely believe that and neither do you. Try your best to make our case wherever, whenever you can, and quickly. You're still with us, Nmadi?"

Ouro smiled. "Of course, Chuma. I had no idea life with you could be so exciting."

They laughed into the wind.

Fasseke said, "We'll get your family off within the week, so don't worry."

"No, Chuma. I know they're in careful hands. But—the Joplin woman . . ."

"Take her with you, Nmadi. Explain things to her. Apologize. Drop her off in Paris. Your flight goes through there. It would not look good to detain her with your special mission, which will continue regardless of what goes on here." Fasseke stopped and deciphered the look in Ouro's eyes. "Me? It's not me they want, Nmadi. It's the plant. The attempt on Shaguri? Didn't work, did it? Come on, man. Aren't you leaving your family in *my* care?" Fasseke slapped Ouro on the back. "Oh, yes. Did Obika speak with you about the book he wants to write?"

Ouro grinned. "Yes. He's a Basil Liddell Hart in the making."

They laughed again, and Ouro thought of the arrangements he'd made with a Lebanese boat captain to remove his family should anything happen to President Fasseke and carry them upcoast to Dakar. Ouro felt guilty, but he also felt a greater sense of ease at having to leave so suddenly. From Dakar they could fly to New York. The Lebanese had asked no questions, had taken the money and quietly folded it and slipped it into his pocket.

"What can he do for us? What has he done for us?" the second secretary and political affairs officer demanded of Klein. "So he knows Fasseke. So he's supposed to have dinner with him. Next *week*. *That* won't do us any good. He arrived when that woman did; he had dinner with her and made that trip to N'Duli, and he picked her up right at my desk and carried her to the hotel. And *she* knows Shaguri very well, or she wouldn't be down here in the first place. So what can Henry do for us, Ken, is what I'm asking. We've got a dozen other people out there."

Klein didn't answer. Instead, he gazed without expression at the second secretary. The second secretary didn't understand that Jake Henry was a diversion, that as in football, he was a decoy drawing linebackers to one hole while the real ball carrier sped through another. That Jake knew there was to be an accident meant nothing. He followed orders.

Now Klein spoke. "Obika's talking to him, taking him on a tour of a barracks."

"Oh, very good," the second secretary said. "Maybe they'll cook each other in pots out there in the bush."

"Didn't know you disliked the man so much," Klein said.

"Hell, *he* shouldn't be *here* in the first place, Ken. You know that. Policy and all that shit."

"He's army. Not one of ours."

"He's a Negro. He's one of *theirs*."

"Creighton, shut up."

"You don't like him any better than I do."

"What's important is that he fits."

The second secretary stared at a map of Pandemi on the wall.

Klein sauntered to the window that overlooked the Avenue of Africa. The cars outside, headlights on, crawled toward Ashmun and Greenville. The wind was lifting and heaving the fronds of the palm trees. There was no sound from the outside; the building was solidly built and sealed for the air-conditioning. So close, Klein thought, but you can't hear anything. He turned back to the second secretary, a thin, heavily tanned man who could've passed for a graduate student. "You'd better get ready for that press conference. A lot of people've drifted over from Temian."

The second secretary sighed. "I'd better get a fat drink, I'm gonna need it." He closed the door quietly when he left.

T E N

Kenneth Klein stood at the window and looked out at Africa. There were only two cities he could abide on the entire continent—Capetown and Nairobi. The rest you could give back to the Africans, the black ones. He knew that things had to fall into place faster and more resoundingly than he first had thought. He was thinking now, he told himself, like a good quarterback would on third and ten, time running out and needing another ten for the touch. No time-outs left and he ignored Coach because he didn't like his choice of plays anymore than Coach liked Klein's.

SOG 1 people in Ulcuma now—and they'd damn well take out their people better than they did in Temian. But you couldn't work without the monkeys; this was their zoo. And where in hell did Fullerton get that fifteen-million-dollar figure from? Hadn't yet learned to discount exaggeration.

One small group of contracts feinting toward Temian. Keep Shaguri on his toes and, if anything broke loose again in his north, something might still work there. Temian monkeys cop the rotors on the choppers. Ulcuma apes dancing on the border to draw Obika from Greboland Barracks and defensive backfield away from Jija. Shaguri's jets useless at night. We sell, but never the whole package. Jake on the border with Obika at 2000, give or take an hour.

SOG 2 people in Swift boats effect landing just outside Jija Deep channel. In (Lawdy me!) blackface. Clear out remaining forces and effect entrance to reactor building and generator. Destroy inlet, outlet conduits, disable both pumps, blow water flow to generator to commence meltdown. Of course an "accident" because the monkeys didn't know what they were doing. There had been extensive discussion as to whether an explosion would result or a "blurble." Everyone came down on the side of "blurble." That was the thinkable. In any case, an accident that disables permanently the Jija Deep reactor. From the moment of complete shutdown until something happened, which fucking ever, there was a 960-second leeway, for SOG to get away. (Good luck, SOG.) Sixteen minutes and ticks.

Fasseke with Shaguri at the Mountaintop, on the flank, isolated.

SOG 3 people here with army and police. Radio Bagui and a quick down-and-out. Announce overthrow. Fasseke in secret deals with Soviets and Chinese. Diversions in the streets near their embassies. Run the cocksuckers into the street. Raiders in: code rooms, operations, anything loose. Take 'em out? Klein guessed no. Chinese and Russian bodies could make a good thing awkward, and this play was gonna work. Klein could feel it in his bones.

Army takes over, dismisses Fasseke. Fast promotions in the Pandemi army!

Jake's death. In the line of duty as an observer. Break up the romance between these monkeys and ours. (Solidarity, no, never.) Nkrumah with an American gorilla advisory group; Malcolm X running around here like an ape in glasses, but he sure got his. And Meredith. Achebe, Ekwensi, Ouro, et al., will get theirs as they move back and forth on the Harlem-Jungle Express. Take the Ape Train. Jake, it's a pass. Monkey go long.

A soft bell rang. Klein looked at his watch. On schedule. He unlocked a bottom desk drawer and pulled out a phone, adjusted some controls on it, and said, "Yes?"

E L E V E N

Now there was not even the somber company of Ebun and Tuzyline. And Iris was not in the suite, but in a dark room that was growing darker with the onset of dusk outside. The window overlooked the backs of buildings. Wooden and cardboard structures leaned crookedly against concrete, brick, and tile. She watched small bursts of flame dot the spaces between the shacks. It was dinnertime. Iris wondered what the people ate, or would eat.

She was not hungry, but she wished Jake would come as he said he would, for dinner. She wanted to talk to him, feel secure in his presence, tell him how very much she just wanted to get out. The conversation with the second secretary had been just routine talk, she feared. She'd heard nothing from him and had gone over his head to the ambassador—only to find that he was not available and, in any case, such matters were routinely the province of the second secretary. Nmadi, too, was not to be found. Oh, Taiwo, she thought. You bastard!

Why *was* it no one seemed to share her distress, her growing fear that she had stepped onto a stage and hadn't learned her lines? And the way they looked at her, as if she were something to be tasted.

Iris settled down to the phone. Every fifteen minutes she settled down to the phone to call the people on her list again. International operator for Taiwo, the American embassy for the ambassador and the second secretary or duty officer; the Pandemi Government House for Nmadi Ouro and the office of the Home Ministry. When she finished this round of calls, with their familiar responses (although there were complaints that the offices were closed) she called room service again and inquired about the whiskey and soda she'd ordered an hour ago. She amended the order this time, boosting it from a double to a triple.

"So," she said aloud. "*This* is Africa!" Then she pounced on the phone once again. She'd forgotten the airlines. "Reservations," she was told, "cannot be honored without an exit visa, miss."

Darkness enfolded her. Iris sat unmoving, listening to the voices along the hotel corridors and those that reached her from the street. They sounded like back home on Saturday night. My people, she thought. Then, *my* people? She battled hopelessness back, turned on the lights, and began to dial again, starting from the top of list.

"You smoke too much!"

"There's nothing else to do!" Bonaco protested.

Akenzua clicked in exasperation and frowned at his

brother, though he knew Bonaco could not see the expression on his face. Akenzua inhaled the wood-burning smell, the charcoal smell, and the odors of a variety of mean foods. He sucked on the kola nut in his mouth. He stretched to peer around the corner of the building. They were sitting on the pavement in the alley between two buildings that faced Jacob Henry's apartment house. There were growths of moss in some places on the wall they leaned against. Akenzua pulled his head back into the alley, and sighing, rolled from one haunch to the other. Not like sitting on plain, soft earth, he thought. Yet, the coming of darkness released him; another day would soon be gone. There could not be too many more. He gazed up at the streetlights and nudged Bonaco and tossed his chin in the direction of the lights. Bonaco looked up. They laughed softly.

"Bonaco."

"What, brother?"

"You should give up all this womanizing. At your age."

"You want me to spend the rest of my life just driving the NOW A PEOPLE IS COMING and sleeping and nothing more?"

"It's not good. And doesn't look good. Old man. Young girls."

"You want me to bring you one, Akenzua?" Bonaco laughed, and the sound of it rumbled smoothly into the darkness. "A joke. A joke. I will tell you, though, if I agree to give them up, you'll come live with me."

"No. You with me," Akenzua said.

The blunt sound of slamming car doors, loud against the sporadic flow of traffic, made them stop talking. They both looked around the corner, "Huh!" Bonaco said.

"It's him," Akenzua said.

Jacob was standing face-to-face with the young white man who often drove him around. Jacob seemed to be angry. The soldier was standing stiffly, sullenly, before him, as though restrained by ropes Akenzua could not see. A movement on the periphery of Akenzua's vision made him look upward to Jacob's balcony. Five flights up, two balconies from the end. In the soft, faded glow of a streetlight, Akenzua saw a man, the man he supposed, who worked for Jacob. Strange man. But why wasn't he leaning out, looking and listening, the way people in other neighborhoods would be doing if they were Pandemis? Why does he hang back like that?

"Jacob seems angry, Akenzua."

"Yes. He's really snapping at that white fellow."

"That car just keeps on running, huh?"

"*Damn* it, Coates. I can *walk*. I don't need a driver now. I don't *want* a driver now." Jake paused because for the first time a thought had come to him that should have come a long time ago. "Tell Klein I didn't want you. Take the sumbitch back, and Coates, that's an order."

"Sir!" Coates shouted. He lunged away from Jake to the car, snatched open the door, piled in, and slammed it shut. He drove off in a scream of wheels and a sweep of headlights. Jake wondered how many people, hidden behind their blinds, had seen them.

He remained motionless, watching the car until he could see it no longer. He was angered not so much by Coates's insistence that he remain to drive, but by what lay behind it. That something was going on was no secret. But, the *when* and *why* were suddenly shifting, or seemed to be. It was not supposed to. He didn't *think* it was supposed to.

He watched the traffic, gazed at the cooking fires he could see sputtering deep in the alleyways behind the buildings. The charcoal smell seemed to be the very air itself. He wondered if he should go up and tell Dawson he wouldn't be having dinner. Hell, if he hadn't been so pissed by the way Coates seemed to want to cling to him, he'd have let the marine drive him right to the hotel.

But Jake had had a lot on his mind after not finding people at the embassy. He'd tried doors, called their offices and Klein at home. It was curious, the two or three new faces that belonged to no particular office, the heavy silence from Klein, the absence of Klein, the second secretary's relationship to Klein, about which Klein had said nothing.

Hey, Jake thought. What, am I here for dinner with Chuma? To share a bit of spit and polish with Obika? By now Klein ought to know that Iris isn't into anything but leaving. Is he pissed there isn't anything more? (Pros don't get mad; they get even.) And what's this Ulcuma shit, the blown takeover in Temian? Oh, he thought, oh. Then, oh, *oh!* Klein's fucked up and he's gotta pull a winner out of the hat *quick.* So he's moved up the schedule for the "accident."

Jake lit a cigarette and felt some of the tension ooze from his body. To hell with Dawson. He started to walk toward the hotel. The charcoal smell made him recall the village, the women cooking. He was getting hungry. And now people were moving about the street. Jake never saw that many during the day in this section of town; it was as though they were at one with the night which hid their poverty. Sound, merry and rambling, flowed about him.

Sometimes it seemed to hush suddenly and then pick up again, back there behind him. The streetlights became bigger and brighter as Jake moved toward the center of town. People gathered, laughing and talking, bouncing and bobbing. They paused in these motions to watch him as he passed, some greeting him, others nodding. Maybe it was the way he walked, or looked; they knew he wasn't one of them. Jake walked on, the tones of their greetings echoing, and then the volume of the voices increased behind him, as though the people had discovered something familiar in their midst. Jake didn't turn. He hurried on to the hotel.

"C'mon up," Iris said on the house phone. "Hurry, 'cause I'm in a hurry." She hung up before Jake could ask what was going on. She sounded happy.

Iris yanked open the door almost as soon as he knocked on it. The room was small and dark; even the lights didn't help; it reminded him of rooms in *pensions* on the Ramblas near the docks in Barcelona.

But she hugged him, came close and hugged him, pressed herself tightly against him, and then fled back to the bed, where she burrowed into a handbag. Her bags were near the door.

"Hey, what's going on? You got the visa? From the embassy? Ouro? You're leaving?"

Iris closed the bag with a snap and a brilliant smile. "Yeah, Jake. I'm leaving. I've got forty minutes. Now, if you grab those bags, we can go downstairs and I'll buy you a drink and tell you all about it. Nmadi's coming. He's on his way to the States by way of Paris. I'm going out with him."

"No!"

"Yes! C'mon, man, let's go."

167

Downstairs, they sat where they could watch the street for the arrival of Nmadi Ouro.

"Sorry you're leaving," Jake said, "but I'm glad you managed it." He wondered why Ouro was leaving the country in a bigger hurry than seemed to have been called for. And, if Chuma knew about Iris and Shaguri, was he now convinced that she was not involved with him, Jake, at least not in the way he must have thought at first? "And I'm sorry we didn't get to spend more time together," Jake said.

Iris studied him through her smile. He seemed less sure of himself than he did just a couple of days ago. She liked him. Pity things had not worked out. But she detested mysteries, especially those that involved her without her knowledge. Taiwo, and now Jake. Paris was safer; she knew her way around there. This was a larger, more impenetrable jungle than she could have ever imagined. "Maybe you'll get to Paris soon," she said. She took his hand. "You want to tell me what's going on, Jake?"

He squeezed her hand. She reminded him of all the girls he'd ever danced with as a boy on the edge of puberty, girls who popped their chewing gum with muted sound as they moved to "After Hours"; girls who smelled of Mum and Tangee powder and lipstick, who accepted the swelling pressure of his body and pressed back against it, calm and regal faces poxed by shimmering dots from the silver globe overhead; girls whose bodies slipped like separate skins on the rayon skirts beneath their dresses, sliding to pause on the beat, then sliding off it; girls with ripe breasts and gently swelling buttocks. Aw, play it, Avery. Girls whose lips rested just beside his, just close enough to suggest other places, other darks. Jake looked at Iris and remembered the movements, the smells, the rhythms, the music. No other woman anywhere, not even his wife, made him remember when he left boyhood and entered his next life.

"Don't ask me that, Iris."

"Okay. Is it bad? Is it going to *be* bad?"

"C'mon."

"But you are."

"What?"

"You know." She didn't want to say it again. Not now.

"Oh, that." Jake glanced at the street. People walked by, their eyes rolled toward the window. Kids pressed to it, stuck out their tongues and ran.

"You don't seem, you know, happy," she said.

"Another drink, Iris. On me." He waved for a waiter.

"All right," Iris said. "I'll leave it alone on one condition."

"Which is?"

"That you tell me about it when you come to Paris."

Jake laughed. "You don't quit, do you, Iris?"

"No."

They hoisted the new drinks. Jake thought about Valerie and the kids. What a mess if they were here. He glanced at his watch. He was really hungry, could eat even one of Dawson's tough steaks. He'd get something when he got back. Dawson didn't do extra hours. "To Paris," Jake said, suddenly missing it more than he ever imagined he would.

"To flight," Iris said brightly.

Nmadi Ouro bustled in behind his driver. His eyes swept the room, fastening upon Iris sitting with Major Henry. Ouro walked to them, side-stepping tables. "Get the bags," he said to the driver. The driver swept up the luggage. "Iris, you're ready?" Ouro asked. "Major, hello."

"Hi, Mr. Ambassador," Jake said. He kept his seat as Iris bounced up. Ouro did not offer his hand.

"I'm ready, Nmadi," Iris said. She glanced from Ouro to Jake and back again.

"Well, then, I suggest we go."

"Okay." She turned to Jake. She wanted to kiss him, but there was that thing in the air she didn't want to disturb.

Jake saw her indecision and said with a smile, "Good trip, Iris."

"See you, Jake."

He watched them leave. From where he sat he could just barely see them getting into the car. He finished his drink and ordered another.

Jake entered his building. It reminded him of a European structure that had been moved, as if by a great capricious windstorm, to Pandemi; that, he realized now, had been his very first impression of it.

He was hungry and he was angry. The drinks, perhaps coupled with Iris's sudden departure, had set these sensations on edge. And he was being followed; clumsily, yes, but followed.

When he entered, Jake pressed the button for the elevator, then slipped around a corner and waited.

"And now?"

Jake recognized Bonaco's voice. He sounded like a man trying hard to keep his temper in check.

"Are you hungry? Are you tired, Bonaco? What do you mean, and now?"

Mr. Fasseke, Jake thought. Uncle Bonaco and Mr. Fasseke. Jesus.

"Well, look!" Bonaco said in a loud whisper. "Here's the elevator, man! And now do we go up and say hello, or do we sit, wait, and watch some more?"

Jake nearly laughed. Two old men trailing him around. They knew something, obviously, but what? And, clearly, they didn't know what to do, yet they must've been concerned with whatever was going on. Jake wondered if his father would have been so protective. No. He hadn't let him breed the habit. Africans were different, the connections longer and stronger. An outsider might sense their presence, but few saw them at work. Jake was, at the moment he stepped softly from around the corner, briefly jealous of all who had membranes to the connection. Indeed, as he smiled at the two startled old men, it seemed that they were, however warped in time, the only connections he had to anything at that very second.

He pretended, though he did not know why that seemed best, surprise as they congealed in the dim doorway light of the elevator. "Mr. Fasseke! Uncle Bonaco! Hello!"

He saw the two men start; their eyes veered quickly toward each other filled with a panic that flattened into a blank sullenness. But Jake, plating his voice with the evenness of innocence, continued. "Have you come to visit?" He gestured to the elevator. "Is Chuma with you, outside?" Gently, he placed his hands on their shoulders, guided them inside, and pressed for his floor even as Akenzua, watching with some uneasiness as the doors groaned shut in protest, said, "Well, we were just taking a walk and decided, you see . . . no, Chuma's not with us . . ."

"After cleaning up the bus—" Bonaco offered.

"I'm glad you came," Jake said. "Now I won't have to eat

171

alone. I can fix some American steaks, and there's some beer, and we can talk."

What can he do, Akenzua asked himself. He remembers to be respectful of his elders. He would not do them any harm.

"Yes, uh-hun," Akenzua said. "I *am* hungry. And you, brother?"

"Ah—yes. Very hungry."

The elevator stopped. "Good, good. Chuma will be pleased that we had the chance to meet again."

Inside the flat, Jake turned on the lights. "Sit down, please. I'll get some beer and get some food out. There's a man who works here, but he's off now." As he went to the kitchen, Jake slipped the telephone pad, which had writing on it, into his pocket. He recognized Dawson's scribbling.

Akenzua wondered where the man was who worked for Jacob; it hadn't been quite two hours ago that he'd seen him in the shadows of the balcony. Akenzua disliked Pandemis who worked as houseboys; that was no work for a man.

"Do you have Tuskers or Star?" Bonaco called after Jake.

"Coming up," Jake called. He pulled out the pad and quickly read: *Call quarterback.* Jesus, Jake thought. Ain't that hip! *Quarterback!* Well, it was true so far; the white boys *were* calling the signals. But Klein could wait, Jake decided. It wouldn't be cool anyway to shoo out Mr. Fasseke and Uncle Bonaco.

Jake brought out a large Tuskers and three glasses, entering the main room as Bonaco was turning on the radio. "It won't be long for the steak," Jake said, passing the beer around. The steaks were barely frozen in the freezer compartment. The refrigerator seemed to have succumbed to the unending moist heat. Back in the kitchen Jake slapped the meat into the broiler and poured himself a stiff Scotch. He carried the bottle back inside. "It won't take—"

"Shhh!" Akenzua said, snapping his finger to his lips. He glared at Jake. Jake looked at Bonaco, who gazed back without expression.

"The fact is," the voice said, "the Americans presume they can control the destinies of nations smaller than theirs; that they can determine which nations will have what and when."

Akenzua held Jake with his eyes.

"That's Chuma," Jake said.

"In the developing world," Chuma Fasseke said, "developing now because underdeveloped and exploited in the past, we see the American government pretending a benevolence that is only to be found in the individual American. I, together with our neighbor and good friend, President Taiwo Shaguri of Temian, determined when I came to this office to help our people and all of Africa that is truly Africa, to select our own destiny. One result of such action was the attack on President Shaguri just days ago. Another is the tired claim of Ulcuma for territory it never owned.

"Why have these things happened now? What do they have in common? Our information is that the Americans wanted to depose President Shaguri, partly to secure, through his replacement, a cheaper price for the oil they purchase. When the attempt on President Shaguri failed, unrest on the Ulcuma border began."

Jake had poured more beer. Now he sipped it, focusing on its amber color, its thready foam. He hurried into the kitchen and turned the steaks, sprayed them with salt and pepper, and returned.

"... far more serious," Chuma was saying. Once again Jake found himself impaled by the glare in Akenzua's eyes.

"The new power plant that only recently brought new lighting to our nation was built with the assistance of President Shaguri and the Temian people. It is a nuclear-powered plant, conceived to be the first in a network of such plants designed to create power for the industry this continent needs and will develop. We will become a giant among giants.

"Of course, the Americans do not want this to happen. It wants all the developing world to be a marketplace for its goods and services—goods Americans themselves don't want, and services that are exploitative. Although there is no evidence that Europeans are involved in the current unrest and the actions of recent days, we do know, however, that their views in the main do not differ greatly from those of the Americans who, after all, are their successors in the plundering of our continent.

"We want to say this: Pandemi and Temian are sovereign states with an African vision of the future. We believe we have friends abroad who support that vision."

Another voice came on. "This has been a repeat of President Fasseke's statement at an unusual press conference called late this afternoon by Foreign Minister Kataka. The president only forty-five minutes ago finished responding to questions from foreign reporters. This has been a special broadcast of Radio Bagui."

Akenzua reached over and turned off the radio.

Jake returned to the kitchen, found plates and utensils, cut up the meat, and brought everything to the table in two wordless trips. "Sit down," he said. Akenzua and Bonaco, as if in deep thought, sidled to the table and pulled up their chairs with sighings and coughings. Jake got another quart of beer and sat down in the silence.

"Good and gracious God," Akenzua intoned, "we thank you for this—" He waited and looked at Jake.

"And all other blessings it has been your graciousness to bestow," Jake said. "Amen."

"Amen," Akenzua and Bonaco said together, their voices bouncing off the plaster walls. Jake wondered if his voice had echoed so much.

Bonaco attacked the meat. Jake and Akenzua eyed each other. Jake passed the Scotch. Both refused. All ate in silence until Akenzua said, "Well, Jacob."

Jake finished chewing. He swallowed and said, "Well, Mr. Fasseke?"

Bonaco poured another glass of beer.

"You heard Chuma," Akenzua said.

"Yes, I heard him."

"It's true about you Americans?"

"Always interfering," Bonaco said. "But Jacob," he said to Akenzua, "isn't an American. He's one of us. They just let him live there until they figure out what they'll do with him."

"Stop, Bonaco," Akenzua said sharply. "Don't be cruel about things beyond a man's ability to change."

"That's all right, Mr. Fasseke," Jake said.

"We know you're not here to help us," Akenzua said slowly. "You're here to help hurt us." He rolled his eyes over at Jake, and Jake gazed back. He wondered how it was that two old men had managed to get hold of something. Klein ought to see this shit, he thought. "And we wonder how this can be, Jacob. We helped to raise you. We knew your father and your mother, so we wonder, though in truth, Jacob, you had in you then what you have in you now. Even so, how is it that you are here and your brothers and our brothers are being beaten and killed in that place you call home? How is it that you do not seem to see the connections between this new war in Asia with so many black men fighting and what you do here—"

Jake interrupted. "I seem to recall a lot of Africans fighting with the French and the British in the great wars, of Africans fighting with the French in Asia, in the same place, and there were Ethiopians in Korea when I was there. I seem to recall that, Mr. Fasseke."

Bonaco waited for his brother's response.

"Uh-huh," Akenzua said, "and that's why it's time to stop making the same mistake, Jacob."

There followed another silence during which they could hear people laughing down in the street.

"Chuma saw the mistakes, Jacob."

"I didn't study philosophy, Mr. Fasseke."

"No," Bonaco said harshly. "You studied to kill. Isn't that a philosophy?"

"Uncle," Jake said, "I guess you're right. It is." To Akenzua Jake said, "It's easy for you to say what's a mistake and what isn't, Mr. Fasseke. I say this without disrespect, but where have *you* been, what have *you* seen, to think *you* know a mistake?"

Akenzua nodded. "You listen to the stories. They are what you call history, uh-huh! You look at things as once they were and as they are now. *You* do not do that, so you can never know mistakes, especially the one you think your father made. What's *going* anywhere and *seeing* everything got to do with what is right and what is wrong?"

"My father's mistake?"

"Not being as strong as you think you are. Not being strong in the way you are. But it takes no strength to kill, to maim the already weakened. It takes strength not to do those things; it takes the iron, Jacob."

Jake saw Akenzua at his forge, arms popping with muscles, pounding iron.

"My father was not betrayed by his country. He was betrayed by his people."

"Because they didn't have to treat him as they did?"

"Exactly, Mr. Fasseke." Jake saw the old men smile at each other; the smile was triumphant.

Akenzua leaned forward. "Uh-huh! Did you just hear yourself, Jacob? Did you hear? They didn't have to, but they did treat your father badly. They could have said, couldn't they, 'No, let's not.' But they did, your father's church people."

"All right," Jake said. "Maybe things weren't going well for them and they were ashamed to say so. I thought of *that*."

"And does one hurt and pass along the hurting, is that it? You accept that as a man's way? No, no, Jacob. And if that was the case, you certainly are not in their situation. Why must you hurt us?"

The walls seemed to be hurling back their words.

Akenzua said, "If it was going badly for the church folk, it probably had to do with your country, where black and white do not worship the same God together, I've been told. At least not very often."

"Like Moslems and Christians," Bonaco said.

"Yes, yes," Akenzua said. "Exactly. So, you cannot blame the black church folk, Jacob. You must blame something else. And that is your country, for which you are here, to do us harm."

"That's not true," Jake said, but his tone floated to the walls and came weakly back to him. And he knew Akenzua heard the lie when he rolled his eyes toward him; they barely concealed a plea. Jake turned away.

Akenzua cleared his throat. "We do not all awake at the same time. Some of us sleep forever, into the grave and beyond. For others there is a wandering in a forest where great trees are marked as signposts. Chuma was lucky. He was wakened, but it is the sleeper that will kill him, or the wanderer, the one who seems awake, but is still with those who lie still." Akenzua leaned back, conscious for the first time that he had piled himself forward on the table. He couldn't tell if Jacob really heard him. He pushed back his chair and it squealed on the tile floor. He stood and as he focused on Jacob, he heard his brother rise too. "It will not be as easy as you think, Jacob."

Jake shrugged, but he felt that his attempt to convey ignorance was as weak as his denial. He looked up at the brothers. They were like a double figure hewn from ebonywood; Bonaco the taller and thinner, Akenzua shorter and wider. A vague similarity was stamped on their faces, and he would have described it as tough.

"Thank you for the food," Akenzua said. "It's the second time you've fed us. Where is your friend, the lady"

"Gone back to Europe, Mr. Fasseke." He watched the brothers turn to the door.

"Your family is well, Jacob?" Akenzua said.

"Yes, sir. Thanks for coming."

Bonaco half-turned and said, "It won't be easy."

"I can see that, whatever it is," Jake said, laughing; but he was thinking, if all you can do is piss in my gas tank and hobble up and down in shadow behind me, it may be easier than you think. "My regards to Chuma," Jake said as he sent them down in the elevator. He stood and listened to it as it whined and groaned downward. Chuma's father hadn't answered.

"Fuck's going on?" Jake asked. He'd called one number and been switched automatically to a second and third.

"What took you so long to get back?"

"Busy."

Nothing came from Klein for seconds. Then he said, "Coates is picking you up at seven to get you to Obika. You do Greboland Barracks tomorrow."

"Not with Coates." The words had come out in a rush that Klein interrupted.

"Yes, Coates. Listen, Jake."

"Listening." Reel it back in, man, reel it in, he told himself. Or you'll wake him up. Klein was still talking. Jake had not heard and so interrupted Klein in turn. "All right, all right. Coates."

"Good," Klein said. "Oh, you know the ambassador's gone to the Cape for a little R and R."

"The Cape?" Then, slowly, he understood. "Cape*town*?" Jake wondered why he was going now. Maybe he wasn't going to be around to cover if they needed him.

179

"Yeah, that's it."

"When do I check back in?"

"Sunday morning, Jake."

"Fine. Look, I've been unable to get in touch with you. Wanna fill me in?"

"Busy. We'll talk Sunday."

When he had hung up, Jake cleared the table, moving slowly and quietly, and when he'd finished, he turned out the lights and drifted to the balcony, where he settled with cigarettes and whiskey. Something gray oozed and puckered in his stomach. He looked down into the street that was almost deserted; only Chuma's streetlights shone flatly down, changing the shadow shapes of an occasional flitting pedestrian. Jake wondered where the two old men were, the old men who dealt in morality and didn't know the game was being played in feet-deep shit. He was caught in it as much as they were.

Klein knew Obika didn't like whites, so why this insistence on Coates's going? Klein had said nothing about the press conference, nothing about calling off "the accident," now that Chuma had told the world about the plant. Even if Klein had somehow arranged to have the broadcasts jammed, there were still the reporters; he couldn't get *all* of them to bury the story, though in general they seemed like an accommodating bunch of drunks wherever they were to be found.

They were Klein's problem. *He* had to think once again of those persistent old men who knew something. From whom did they get it? From where? What precisely did they get? Jake thought of Africans sitting around their fires in forests and villages, in city homes, this night as well as all other nights. Families, mothers and daughters, fathers and sons.

And why wouldn't they have talked? *Jacob* was coming back. Jacob, who had been son, brother, nephew. Jacob, who knew Chuma, who knew Chuma had loved Miriam in and out of his boyhood. Jacob, who happened to arrive just exactly, precisely, at the time the new plant became operational.

Everyone thought Africans were dumb, or everyone just didn't give a damn about what Africans did and thought. Jake cursed Klein and his operations. Klein's people were always looking down on everyone else's operations; Klein's people got the press, the bucks, the golden whispers; his people were everywhere the army was still getting to, and when the army did arrive, Klein's people were there to meet them on the beach with champagne that had gone flat. Like now.

I should've said no, Jake thought.

T W E L V E

The crimson, lime, and gold-colored wagon labored up the slight hill. It wobbled and blue smoke billowed from its rear. It was crowded, inside and on the running boards, with, Jake assumed, the same people who rode it every morning at this time. There were no people waiting on the corner this morning, so the NOW A PEOPLE IS COMING continued on its way, shaking and groaning to the crest and down the gentle slope toward the Ashmun Hotel.

At least, Jake thought, he knew where Uncle Bonaco was this morning.

"Chop ready, sah," Dawson called.

Jake left the balcony. He surveyed the table and said, "Looks good, Dawson." The bacon was crisp; the eggs looked soft, and the coffee smelled just right.

"I see bag packed, sah. You go 'way?"

"Yeah."

"Back when, sah, so I fix chop?"

"Sunday morning, Dawson."

Dawson grinned. "You eat steak last night, sah? With other people, huh?"

"Yeah, it was good. Better get some more from the embassy, okay?"

Dawson bobbed his head. "I get, sah. Sure."

"Dawson, you a Mano?"

Dawson's grin split the air between them. "Yes, sah! How you guess that?"

Jake laughed. "Just a guess, that was it."

Dawson said, "You see, sah, the more you stay in Pandemi, the more you see the different peoples."

Jake was pleased that Dawson had emerged, however briefly and for whatever reason, from his sullen shell. Someone had told him, somewhere (he now forgot), that Africans the continent over did not especially like to serve African-Americans. As he ate, Jake thought to cement this new relationship; he would give Dawson a pack of American cigarettes before he left.

On the balcony, to which he returned, still savoring his breakfast, done close to the perfection a condemned man dreamed of but never got, Jake lit up and watched the traffic build along the street. The mist that enveloped this section of Bagui with its dampness was easing. It would blow the creases in his tans. He supposed that Chuma knew these sea mists, that they hampered him not one bit.

He watched the traffic building and thought of the traffic in Paris Iris must be listening to, half-asleep, gratefully clutching the bed in which she slept. Her apartment would be in such a section, where traffic hummed. In Maryland it was already past noon, and he wondered what Val was doing, free from the kids who were now in school. Silver Spring. Shit. He would take Paris any day, any night. Yes, he would.

The silver mist was lifting now, in globs, like gossamer dumplings, and beneath it, as if in sinister purpose, there rolled the car, sparkling, firm, and with a heaviness that made the occasional Citroëns and Fiats look like toys. Jake watched Coates slide out, check the street, lock the car, and enter the building. Jake had grabbed his bag and was on the way out when the buzzer sounded.

"Morning, sir," Coates said. A smile bulged on his wide flat face. He took Jake's bag, unlocked the trunk, and placed it carefully inside. Jake barely glimpsed Coates's own bag, a case just the right size for a Uzi, and what appeared to be, as Coates briskly lowered the trunk lid, a PRC-77 radio.

"Hello, Sergeant. Hot already, eh?" Jake slipped on his sunglasses and thought about the Uzi. The story was that the South Africans had blackmailed the Israelis into making the gun available. But the Israelis, fearing the loss of friends—as well as considerable financial support from South African Jews whose funds would no longer reach Israel if the South Africans didn't get the gun—brought in Herstal as a third party, let them license the gun. Now the goddamn thing was turning up in the damnedest places.

"Yes, sir," Coates said. "Soon's that mist burns off it gets hot. Say, listen, Major. I'm sorry about last night. I got carried away—"

"Okay, Coates," Jake said. They were talking over the top of the car. He didn't want to hear what Coates had to say. He just wanted a couple of answers. "We're getting transport at Obika's office?"

"Change of orders, sir. We go right up in this baby. In style." Coates grinned. "And in comfort. Obika had to go up last night, and he preferred our coming via our own transport, in case he had to stay. We'll meet him there."

Jake flicked a bug off the top of the car. Generals liked to send cars, make use of the troops. Jake nodded. They were changing plans like he wasn't even in the game. He studied Coates. They were dressed alike, in short-sleeved tans, boots, and cap. "I'm glad somebody can tell me what the fuck's going on," Jake said, climbing into the front seat. There he noticed for the first time that the American flags were in their sockets, hanging limply. The trip was going to be very official, which further puzzled him because generally the rule was very low visibility. "What's with the flags?"

Coates slid into the driver's seat. "Ambassador's orders."

"The ambassador's away."

"Came down before he left, sir. All embassy vehicles are to fly the flag until further notice."

You flew the flag when things were happening or about to happen; they let everyone know you were Uncle Sam's nephew and not to be fucked with; you were an American national, a member of that great, benevolent peacekeeper, even if peace was the least of your professions.

As they eased into the thickening traffic, rolled down past the Ashmun, Jake unfolded a map and laid it on his lap. They would be going northwest; north northwest, to be exact. The Greboland Barracks was not far from Jija Near and the Ulcuma and Temian borders. There are no coincidences in this business, Jake thought. Without looking up he asked, "What're your orders, Coates?" He felt the marine glance at him.

"To drive you there, serve as your aide, and to get you back Sunday morning, sir." He paused. "And to follow your orders, naturally."

"Hmmm," Jake said pleasantly. "Are you armed?"

"I have a pistol, sir. We double as bodies on these assignments. That goes without saying, Major. That's what got me upset last night."

Jake turned full around and laughed. He could not stop laughing. Coates at first smiled, then chuckled, then frowned. "What's funny, sir?"

Jake shook his head as his laughter died. "Nothing," he said. He was glad he had packed his own pistol, an oldie but goodie Walther P-38. If you put in a little effort, you could still find them in Germany, some even with the swastika stamped on them.

They were already out of the city and the unpaved road was just ahead. Jake sighed and rolled up his window. Coates rolled his up, too, and flicked on the air-conditioning. "Here we go," he said, and dirt and small stones began to rain and rasp against the underside of the car; vehicles began to approach them through tunnels made by cascading red dirt.

They passed a great, cleared area filled with milling people, ramshackle stalls, tethered goats, and caged guinea fowl.

"Not what you'd call a stateside supermarket, huh, Major? That's the Bagui Road marketplace."

"No," Jake said. He felt both defensive and embarrassed. He stared at the people with huge parcels on their heads, the furious bargainers, the dirty livestock. The market was a hundred times larger than the one he remembered from the village. He said without turning to Coates, "Most of the people in the world live like this, Sergeant. Most of them." But he was relieved when, finally, they swept past.

Here the land was savannah, as if drained of the sea a thousand years ago. But toward the east, a great distance away beyond the infrequent coconut palms, was a firm green tree line. According to the map, there would be rain forests in Greboland.

Jake pulled his cap down over his eyes and rested his head back on the seat. He wondered if Val was getting settled in okay, if the kids liked going to school in the States. What, he wondered, would it be like out of the army. What could he do? Which contacts could he work if he resigned? Couldn't he do at least these last four years? He turned away so Coates could not see his smile. Val sure would be happy if he quit—but wouldn't be happy if he couldn't support them. She was as used to the army as he was, whatever its faults. He could get sent to Vietnam after this; no doubt about that. There, he might even, quickly, make the star. He'd have to expose his ass again and he knew he couldn't move as quickly as he had sixteen years ago. He didn't want to be a hero anymore; he just wanted to stay alive. He wasn't even mad at his father any longer. Jake sat up and pushed back his cap and listened to that thought echo from side to side in his head.

The flags rippled and snapped. Jake thought of the very first time he'd heard of the colors in Amsterdam, during a Fourth of July parade when little kids behind him whispered as a proud color guard passed smartly by (how well soldiers looked on parade!). "Red, white, and blue! Yer father is a Jew! Yer mother is a Polack, and so are you!" Snapping and rippling in Africa.

The sun, still climbing up in the east, rolling up above the tree line, glared fiercely against his window, bored in with its heat. Jake turned toward Coates and slipped down on his neck. He pulled down the bill of his cap again and closed his eyes. "We should be there about fifteen hundred?"

"Closer to sixteen hundred, Major."

Jake could open his eyes and see Coates; the marine, however, Jake realized, could not see that Jake, beneath his cap and behind his sunglasses, had a clear field of vision. He could study Coates, who probably knew more about what was going down than he. Good, Jake thought, and promptly began to ponder a way to relieve the marine of the Uzi, if necessary. He thought it would be necessary. Coates pressed a switch and the wipers came on, whispering back and forth and clearing temporarily the settling dust from the windshield.

The timing, as usual, was perfect. The car and the accompanying jeeps had not finished braking before Shaguri's helicopter hammered in above the trees and landed in a hurricane of dust. Few people, even having observed the craft coming in, had time to see President Chuma Fasseke leave his car and, with head lowered, walk quickly beneath the blades and grasp the outstretched hand of Manoah Maguru.

Fasseke waved once to Pendembou, who with Lieutenant Mbundi and another soldier had climbed out of the car to watch the takeoff. Mbundi saluted. Fasseke watched them, the car, the jeeps, shrink sharply as the craft rose as if sucked upward by its own thunder; it tilted and angled in the west, Fasseke saw the blue-bright sea. Maguru snapped the last belt around him as the sea straightened, roads and structures became defined; groves of coconut palms and rubber trees became grids within shapeless green; it all fell away and behind the thundering machine that was carrying Fasseke to his meeting with Shaguri.

The small convoy moved off before the dust settled on the landing area. Abi Pendembou, in the rear seat, opened his snakeskin case and removed papers and a pen. He plunged into his work behind the khaki-clad backs of Mbundi and the driver.

The lead jeep plowed dust back toward the car; the car sent dust billowing back toward the trailing jeep; the car rumbled and shook. Pendembou worked on. About fifteen minutes later, Pendembou suddenly raised his head; an alarm had gone off inside him. They were not on the hard road as they should have been. Some measure of time, distance and place, having been computed in his brain after so many of these trips, had gone awry. Pendembou saw dense growth and realized they were on Plantation Road, the long way back to the city, the way with few travelers. He was seized with indignation. How could this broken Mbundi make such a decision, delaying the return so that Pendembou would be unable to call the Mountaintop on schedule?

"Mbundi!" Pendembou cried. "Why have we come the long way?"

Even as he asked, he knew the answer, and there was no answer from Mbundi, who touched the soldier's arm. The soldier tapped the horn twice. The jeep ahead slowed, seemed to creep through the dust and then turned into the undergrowth, the car following, the jeep behind following it, the soldiers beside the drivers in both vehicles pointing rifles at the car.

"Return to the road at once, Lieutenant!" Pendembou shouted.

As Mbundi turned to him, a pistol in his hand, Pendembou was aware of limbs and twigs lashing and snatching at the car.

"Blow the horn," Mbundi said.

The driver hit the horn once.

The jeeps stopped. The foliage was so thick that it lay on and against the car, thumped it.

In the abstract it was neat and clean and in the realm of a fantasy that after all might not occur. But the moment the car stopped, Pendembou felt his bladder go.

"Give me that," Mbundi said, grabbing for the papers and the case, not without the quick tracking of fear over his face. "Get out."

Abi Pendembou made a mute appeal to the driver, whose face was expressionless. His eyes danced from Pendembou to Mbundi and briefly, Pendembou saw, there was that dull light in them of the drugged bull-dancer trying to vault over the weight of his history. Pendembou opened the door on the driver's side, slapped at Mbundi's gun hand, and leaped into the brush in almost a single motion. He was surprised by the hardness, the strength, of Mbundi's hand, startled by the force of the steaming heat into which he plunged, amazed at the pungency of the dull, heavy odor of a thousand year's rotting vegetation. His traditional Pandemi robe caught on the door's edge and on the bushes. He struggled. He saw no other sudden movements, heard nothing but the million-year-old sounds of Africa. Caught, Pendembou whimpered, perhaps hoping in the ancientmost of his brain cells that having done so, having signaled absolute fear, complete defeat, he would be spared, but that was the moment they shot him, emptying their guns into his traditional Pandemi robe.

The helicopter landed within the great circle of parked, camouflaged vehicles, its blades beating down the grasses. Manoah Maguru bounded lightly out, then wheeled and grasped Fasseke to aid him to the ground. The soldiers within Fasseke's vision, all heavily armed, saluted; Fasseke returned the salute.

He had not often been to the Mountaintop; he'd never wished to be indebted to Shaguri for more than he already was. True, Shaguri's retreat was on Pandemi land, and Shaguri had offered Fasseke an almost similar site (the highest point in Temian was only 900 feet above sea level), with structures to be built according to Fasseke's specifications, but Fasseke declined. There was already far too much ostentatious living for the very few in Africa, and he neither wanted nor needed such a place.

Behind them the helicopter blades rushed and whistled to a stop. Before them came Shaguri, clad in one of his Parisian-made safari suits; yards away, Shaguri flung wide his arms and held them there until they were close enough to embrace. To Fasseke he looked troubled and wan, chastened and weary.

"Come, Fasseke, there's much to discuss."

"I'll go and monitor Mr. Pendembou's signal, sir," Maguru said to Fasseke.

Shaguri and Fasseke, at a slower pace, followed Maguru

into the house. Inside, Shaguri led Fasseke to a room with great glass doors. Fasseke gazed into the distance, imagined Ulcuma's borders nestled like the point of a knife between Pandemi and Temian. But all was bright green and dark, stark brown sheltered by blue sky that was barely hinting a darkness at its edges. Fasseke could also see the cars, jeeps, reconnaissance cars, the helicopter, and the soldiers in their camouflage dress.

Shaguri gestured to a sofa. "Sit down, Fasseke, my friend, sit down, sit down."

Fasseke sat, letting himself melt into the cushions, his eyes still fixed to the outside which had smelled of hot grass, oil, gas, and sunburnt metal. Inside, it smelled of Shaguri's cologne. Shaguri poured two tall glasses of lime juice, handed one to Fasseke, and sat down across from him.

"How are you?" Fasseke asked.

Shaguri made a lip-smacking noise over his drink and sighed. "Well, let me tell you. Not as ignorant as the day the Jija Deep plant opened. I can certainly tell you that!"

"A lot—too much—has happened in just a few days, that's true. But where are we now, Shaguri? The Americans have been very active in Pandemi."

Shaguri snorted. "At least you haven't been shot at!"

"I didn't know that," Fasseke said.

"You can talk misery into a disease," Shaguri said. "So I didn't mention it." He drank. "I was huddled under my desk for nearly half a day, Fasseke, and all the time, bang-bang-bang. But it's over. As long as you have Obika you won't have the problem I did. Oh, I was lucky, let me tell you, Fasseke, and I have to tell you there were moments under that desk when I wondered if we were crazy to have done it."

Fasseke felt a sudden fright. "Yes?"

Shaguri shrugged. "Of course we were right to have done it." His short laugh was without resonance. "It suddenly seemed wise when Kehinde rescued me, immediately to raise the wages of the police and the army. Then, of course, I had to have the mutineers executed, to teach everyone a lesson." Shaguri leaned forward. "The Americans would call that putting sugar on the shit."

Fasseke sipped slowly and looked glumly at the troops outside.

"If necessary, Shaguri, can you commit any troops to me?"

"Do I *dare*, my friend? The truth is, in the north, those bloody goddamn Hausas have not quit! Kehinde's got soldiers there right now. They don't give a damn about nuclear power plants or African unity. They'd like an all-Moslem Africa! Ramadan every day! Their legacy to us was not only slavery, though we had the same as today—too many greedy Africans—but Islam. I tell you, man, I'm weary of doing rituals, here this thing and there that thing. As far as I'm concerned, God spits on all religions."

Fasseke waited for Shaguri's anger to subside. Then he said, "It is our plant, Shaguri."

"I know. I have not said it was impossible."

Fasseke looked out again, the sun was starting to ease down in the west. They turned at Maguru's footstep. Maguru's eyes were fixed on Fasseke. "There was nothing from Pendembou, so I tried to reach him, sir. There was no answer."

"No answer?"

"I tried several times, sir."

"Kataka, try Kataka."

"I did, sir. Same thing."

Fasseke and Shaguri, now on the edges of their seats, exchanged glances.

"We're monitoring Radio Bagui. Everything's normal so far."

"Manoah," Shaguri said curtly. "Tell Owalowo to alert the squadron, and to get a helicopter over Jija Deep and the Ulcuma border."

"I believe he's already done that sir."

Shaguri smiled. "Good. Then ask Kehinde to establish contact with General Obika at the Greboland Barracks. Let us know when that's been done."

Maguru inclined his head and left.

Seconds after his departure, Fasseke looked outside and saw an officer with a radiophone to his ear. One second after that he was shouting (Fasseke could tell by his movements and from the reactions of the men), and soldiers stopped strolling and fanned out away from the house, their weapons held at the ready.

Fasseke stood, adrenaline pumping.

"I'd better get back, Shaguri. Now."

Shaguri stood. "No. Wait. Listen. It may be nothing. But if it is, Pendembou and Kataka are not military men." Shaguri broke off to glance at the sky; the west was still ablaze with light; the east's shadows were growing. "Sit back down, my friend, and wait. If this present is to end, we still have a future, though God knows how long, and we'll need someone to bear us into it. Sit."

Fasseke sat and wrapped a silence around himself.

"Where is Ms. Joplin?"

Fasseke was surprised to hear himself answering in civil tones. "She is in Paris. Ouro took her out on his way to Washington."

Shaguri sighed. "Thank you. Sorry about that, my friend."

"Yes. It was somewhat awkward. We weren't sure about her."

"Because of the American?"

"Yes." Fasseke thought of his wife, and then of his father. "About the American . . . we don't know how he fits in."

Shaguri, too, was closely watching the movements outside. "Maybe his history has overtaken him, Fasseke. As you know, all people there are not equally Americans, as people here are not equally Pandemis or Temians, yet, for different reasons, of course."

"I know, Shaguri." Fasseke thought of Yema again. "Do you have any regrets?"

"No. Do you?"

Fasseke thought. "Not concerning what we've done. My regrets are for a world where this can happen, but then history told us it was bound to."

"That's why we prepared."

Fasseke chuckled. "Yes, like an ant scuttering before the harmattan." He turned before Shaguri's scowl; Shaguri, he knew, was thinking of the great amounts of money his nation had invested in Jija Deep, of the Blue Squadron. Fasseke said, "But insects like the ant are or can be pernicious."

"You sound like it is at the end, Fasseke; there is no end, only stages."

"No, no, my good friend," Fasseke said. "I am merely bemused and sorrowed that it will take Africans so long to learn of this, if it is to come, this end. Now, don't tell me that you would want all this to slide under the consciousness of this continent, as though it hadn't happened at all; that you don't want seeds to have been cast about, ready to take root at the first opportunity?"

Shaguri sighed. "You're right. I do want this to have counted for something if, *if* it doesn't—" He broke off as Maguru returned.

"Sir," Maguru said to Fasseke. "General Obika's moved a battalion closer to the Ulcuma border. He's commanding." He looked at Shaguri. "Mr. President, General Kehinde's able to send a company, no more. He says he's in the process of decimating the rebels in the north and still must watch the cities. There is, however, no great problem."

Shaguri tapped his glass against his teeth. "Why are the troops here being deployed, Manoah?"

"Just a precaution, sir. Nothing more." Maguru waited.

"Yoo, Manoah?" Shaguri watched as Fasseke got up and began to pace. "Yes?"

"The rotors on all the helicopters have been made inoperable, sir."

Shaguri stood, his feet slamming the tiled floor. "How? By whom? When?"

"No one knows, sir."

"Replace them!"

"They've already begun, sir, but the work will take"— Maguru glanced at the paper in his hand—"twelve hours, sir."

As one they all turned; the shadows were now very long and very black.

"Radio Bagui?" Fasseke said. "Kataka? Pendembou?"

"Nothing."

"Jija Deep?"

"Well protected, sir. And radar reports nothing untoward."

"Blue Squadron?" Fasseke said.

"No need for it now," Shaguri said softly. "My fear is that whatever may happen will occur at night. Then we can't use it at all." He touched Maguru on the shoulder. Maguru left.

Shaguri eased himself back into his seat. He smiled at Fasseke. "I am sorry, Chuma, for all that's happened that may have been my fault."

Fasseke signaled with his hand that it was all right. He knew Shaguri was waiting for something only he, Fasseke, could now give him. Fasseke said, "The option, Taiwo?"

Shaguri seemed to sigh, but Fasseke heard no sound.

"Is there anything else, my friend?"

Fasseke studied once again the scene outside the window. "No," he said. "No, there isn't. I'll order shutdown at once. But that won't stop them from destroying Jija Deep."

"I know. But at least they won't destroy this corner of Africa for our people. But let Obika and Kehinde make them pay. They must pay."

Fasseke shrugged. "The world will never know of it."

"We will know," Shaguri said. "The world doesn't care and if it did, it would prefer that we did not have Jija Deep."

Shaguri watched Fasseke stand. "Come," Fasseke said. "Let's have Maguru put through the calls for us."

Shaguri stood. "Ahh, Chuma." His feet seemed rooted in the floor.

197

"Come on," Fasseke said. "We have to do it."

"I know. But it was such a good plan. Time, money, hopes, the future . . ."

"It's still a good plan. Maybe we are just a bit ahead of our time?"

Shaguri said, "We have no time left, Chuma, unless they destroy each other." He pulled at his jacket. "Well, let's do it."

THIRTEEN

A Pandemi army truck sat across the road, a machine gun, pointing skyward, mounted in its rear. Coates braked to a stop, cursing softly under his breath. Jake came erect. Coates had said he was armed, but his pistol was in the trunk. Loose terminology; the gun was near, was all, and if Jake read his sergeant right, his race was as effective as a weapon. Until this moment.

A short sergeant hopped down from beside his driver and approached as Jake and Coates got out of their car. The Pandemi sergeant saluted Coates. Embarrassed, the marine stepped aside and gestured to Jake, who was relieved to observe that the two soldiers in the rear of the truck did not unhinge the gun and point it at them. The soldiers were very young and they were trying to look tough.

"I am Major Henry," Jake said. "Anything wrong? Oh, this is *Sergeant* Coates."

The Pandemi sergeant offered a flustered salute. Jake did not return it. "I'm attached to the embassy of the United States, Sergeant," Jake said. Beside him it seemed that Coates was trying to emphasize his height and his bulk, the way a DI might before recruits. "We have an appointment with General Obika."

The Pandemi sergeant squinted up at Jake. "Routine patrol, sir, on the approaches to the barracks. You can proceed to the gate. Five miles straight ahead on this same road."

The sergeant saluted again and barked a command to the driver of the truck; the vehicle was backed off the road. This time Jake returned the salute. The Pandemi soldiers stared as Coates and Jake got back inside the car.

"Whew," Coates said. "You just can't tell what these guys have in mind when they come up like that." He drove slowly past the truck, his eyes glued to the rearview mirror. When they had gone about two miles, Coates pulled over quickly. "I'm gonna strap on, Major."

"I gotta piss anyway," Jake said, but Coates was moving quickly toward the trunk of the car. Jake slid out and went to the front and opened up. The moment the trunk lid was up, blocking Coates's view of him, Jake crouched and plunged a blade from his Swiss army knife into the tire, gave it a vicious twist, closed the knife, jammed it back into his pocket. He was upright urinating when Coates slammed shut the lid.

"That feels good," Jake said, his urine smashing and spattering the hard dry earth.

"Yeah, me too," Coates said. He turned his back to Jake and began to urinate.

For a couple of moments, aside from the hot wind sifting through the trees, and the birds crying in flight, the only sound was of urine making a tattoo on the ground that refused to absorb it.

"Shit," Coates said when they were inside the car. "It won't work."

The .45 in its holster was just too big for Coates to sit comfortably with it on. The marine seemed to be nervous. "Put the piece on the seat, Sergeant," Jake said. He turned away; he didn't want to see the look of indecision in Coates's eyes. If the marine tried to drive with the gun between his legs, that would reveal something Coates didn't yet want known; if he placed the gun on the seat between them, there was nothing to be revealed. Coates dropped the gun on the floor next to his left leg. "I'm guarding you, Major—"

"Protecting?" Jake asked.

"Yeah, that's what I meant to say." Coates laughed and they drove on.

The tire went flat within sight of the entrance to the Greboland Barracks.

"Shit!" Coates shouted, slapping the steering wheel with his palm and directing a swift, hooded look of accusation at Jake.

They got out, Coates slipping his pistol into its holster. They stared at the tire. Jake said, "That's flatter'n shit, Sergeant. Go tell those guys at the gate who we are, why we're here, and that we need some help."

"Aw, I can fix the tire, Major."

Jake glanced at his watch, then up at the sky. "We're running late, Coates. It'd be wise to have them call the general and tell him why."

Coates hesitated.

"I'll watch the car, Sergeant."

Coates reached inside and took the keys.

Jake laughed low in his throat and held out his hand. "Leave the keys, for chrissake; don't make it *that* obvious that you don't trust them. This isn't what you think Harlem is."

"Oh," Coates said, unable to think quickly of a reason why he should keep the keys. "Yeah." He tossed them to Jake with a slow, almost sad, underhand motion. He pulled on the peak of his cap and began to march the quarter mile to the gate, where four soldiers, now stationing themselves several yards apart, watched them, their rifles held in that casual position of the rifleman who is well trained.

Jake scanned the ground that was beginning to weigh heavily with shadows, and he saw in that first scanning part of a shattered tree limb, and picked it up. He stepped to the trunk of the car, watching Coates, whose walk had become tough, like a new kid on the block trying to establish a rep. The Pandemi soldiers watched without expression. Jake opened the trunk lid, his eyes darting from Coates's back to the inside of the trunk. He grabbed his bag and opened it; he opened the case with the Uzi that was jammed in a corner and took out the gun and two box cartridges. Jake put the piece of wood into the case. Coates hadn't turned. Jake closed the lid softly, leaned against it until it closed with a dull snap.

The Africans saw something, Jake thought. Let 'em wonder what it was they saw, whether good for them or not; or maybe in some strange way they wanted him to succeed, whatever the venture.

Coates, his usual loping walk now shortened into the cautious steps of a combatant, had just reached the line of soldiers when Jake yelled. "Sergeant!" Jake began to trot.

Coates seemed to be relinquishing, through his gestures, his prerogatives of race; the grins fled from the faces of the soldiers, the ones that had appeared in response to Jake's yell, and were replaced instantly with the expressions the curious display at the sight of a thing never seen before.

Jake trotted on, aware of the shadows, the dust kicking up under his booted feet; Jake was completely aware of Coates's relief, his pleasure that he could at this instant display in Jake's person the possibilities of America.

"Once they reach General Obika," Jake said, pleased that he was not breathing especially hard, "I'd better get right on in. Catch up with me after you see about that tire." Jake whipped the keys to Coates. "Make sure these guys don't fuck with the car. Say, Coates. You might want to radio back and let the DO know where we are, right?" Yeah, sucker. I know you got it.

Jake stepped forward to present himself and his driver.

A jeep came hurtling down the road toward them as the Pandemi corporal with the oversized British army stripes—turned upside down—was finishing the cigarette Jake had given him. One soldier lounged beneath the shade of the guardpost; he sneaked frequent glances at Jake. The other two were crouched with Coates beside the flattened tire. Coates looked mean, and he was working feverishly, Jake thought, as though he must not miss anything that might happen. Tough, Jake thought, tough that he knows I know about that radio; and even if he had checked the bag with the Uzi and found the gun gone, that, too, would have been tough and too late.

Jake welcomed the arrival of the jeep at the gate of the

fifteen-foot-high fence which ran out of sight on both sides. The corporal's English wasn't too good. The driver, a small, sharp-faced man who wore captain's bars, saluted as he braked and wheeled the vehicle back in the direction it'd come from. With the engine running, he shouted, "Captain Tubman, sir. General Obika would like you to join him in a surveillance of the Ulcuma frontier, Major Henry."

Jake returned the salute and started for the jeep. He ignored Coates, who was walking quickly toward them.

Tubman slammed the gearshift into first, balanced his feet on brake and clutch. "The corporal will assign a man to guide you in, Sergeant. To headquarters. Then you'll get transport and join us." The jeep dug in as they sped away, leaving Coates and the soldiers watching. Fifteen minutes, Jake thought. He'll have it fixed in fifteen minutes. "Sorry we're late," Jake said to Captain Tubman.

"It's nothing. The general went up hours ago. He thought this would be more interesting than just a drive through the camp."

"Problems up there?"

"I don't believe so, sir." Tubman's accented English was like Obika's: clearly English, but with rumbles, dips, and flourishes, speeds and bursts that were rooted in the way Jake remembered Africans speaking.

It was not so much what Tubman said, but the way he said it that made Jake conclude that the captain didn't want to talk.

Jake smelled the sea smell; it floated in between the smell of the dust, the smell of the forest through which they rode at breathtaking speed. Jake glimpsed parade grounds, rows of gray buildings, groups of soldiers. Tubman, Jake had noticed, was wearing an AUS .45. Jake turned half around and opened his bag. Feeling around the Uzi, he found the Walther and pulled out the belt, holster, and gun. He strapped it on; the gun dangled nicely over the side of his seat; one of the good things about jeeps. He ignored Tubman's flickering eyes; he wanted him to see the gun.

"Whenever he arrives, bring him to me. Yes, bring him directly to me, wherever I am." That was what Obika had told Tubman, and this order weighed heavily upon him.

Jake mashed down, hard, instinctively, as Tubman, punching the horn, swerved around a group of soldiers playing on the road. But there was a soft, slick thud. Tubman didn't stop; he didn't turn. Neither did Jake; he bent beneath the windshield and lit a cigarette. Tubman kept double-clutching and shifting and Jake realized that they'd been driving uphill, to a plateau; that's why it seemed cooler.

Jake thought about the soldier Tubman had hit. Was there any doubt? But there had not been a single outcry from the others. What kind of training could that imply, or was it plain old subservience? Then he recalled the story in Korea about an officer shooting dead a young soldier who'd caved in weeping and crying. But here, the Grebomen were supposed to be the thinkers, the intellectuals. Jake tried to envision an army in which the officers' contempt for the men could result in victories. This was the stuff of mutinies. He could not imagine that Obika was like Tubman.

Now off to the west, between the blackening trunks of the trees and their limbs and branches, which were beginning to sway with a growing wind, Jake saw glimpses of the distant sea. They continued at high speed across the intersection of a road that ran off to the east and west. The Pandemi captain was giving his full attention to the road. Abruptly, out of the darkening east came a thunderous crescendo of sound that seemed to be aimed right at them and, even as Jake ducked, he knew it was a jet smashing along the sky. Jake's fear had come and gone as swiftly as the plane. It whined and whickered, trailing behind it a sharp whistling sound and banked out on the horizon to return. As it did, higher in the sky, another jet howled out of the east, banked high in the west, took a wing position on the first, and they roared back to the east. Tubman had said nothing.

They had been driving along a plateau after cresting the incline into the camp, and now Tubman slowed as the jeep began to nose slightly downward. The captain shifted into a lower gear. Jake wondered why he hadn't yet put on the headlights. Ahead he saw at the edge of the road a guardpost and a barrier. Tubman stopped at the guardpost, set the hand brake, and shifted into neutral. Two soldiers approached and saluted as he leaped out and began talking in a language Jake could not understand. One of the soldiers dashed for the phone, the other to open the barrier as Tubman vaulted back into the jeep. "I told them to expect your sergeant and also to call ahead and tell General Obika that we won't be long." Tubman grinned. "Relax, Major. I drive as good as the Americans, don't I?"

Jake grunted, he grunted at precisely the same time he thought he heard small-arms fire, brief, uncertain volleys, far down ahead of them. "Night maneuvers, Captain?"

"No. Most likely Ulcumans having fun with our border patrols."

"And that's where the General is."

"Yes, sir."

Jake no longer minded not having the headlights on.

"The guards back there had been called. Your sergeant is about a quarter of an hour behind us. Made good time, didn't he?"

"Sure did," Jake said. "But I thought he would. I hope he doesn't run over any more of your people."

Tubman was driving more slowly. He said, "That would be bad."

Hey, Jake thought. Wait a minute, Jim. Was he saying that he didn't care if Coates mashed another Pandemi soldier on the road? Jake had heard of such things, people being splattered as if they were insects, by tanks, planes, artillery and, yes, ground vehicles rushing here and there. He had read of them everywhere, and excused them, more or less, in a war, and perhaps even laid such reports to Western press exaggeration when they were said to have occurred in places like Kenya and the Congo. But what was he to believe when whispers were emerging from Vietnam? There were those abstract projections, he supposed, but he'd never been close to one or a witness to that kind of abstraction which, finally, was not an abstraction at all. And he'd never known a participant until now. It was somehow different, or even okay, when you did it to the enemy. But to your own people? Jake could even, with strain, understand the Frightened Irish in The Crater; he could not understand this.

The gunfire racketed closer. Tubman, crawling along now in first gear, turned off to a narrower road tucked behind a ridge. Ahead, Jake saw dim lights.

"This it?" Jake asked.

"Yes, sir."

Jake hoisted his bag to his lap. The velocity of the wind had increased. Behind the ridge, the gunshots sounded faint, like the popping of damp firecrackers on a string. Tubman flashed his lights, bursting the darkness and then burrowing deeper into it. Jake sensed, indeed, somehow *knew* that they were being tracked by sound and perhaps even by sight. These men would have good night vision.

"Captain Tubman?"

The voice was not quite a command.

"Tubman," the captain answered, stopping abruptly and turning off the ignition. "With the American Major Henry."

Lights splashed over them. Jake heard, above the wind, the squeaking of wood and metal against dry hands. Jake gazed around but saw nothing but hot bright light against whose glare Tubman seemed to struggle from the jeep. "In then," Tubman said, and Jake, his hand wet against the straps of his bag, followed. Tubman was waiting the way a guard waits for a prisoner to step out before him. Tubman pointed and Jake stumbled toward the base of the ridge, emerging step by step, from the center of the glare until he could see a ring of soldiers around them.

"The general's waiting."

Jake recognized the voice; it was the one that had called out Tubman's name. Jake thought he saw a few vehicles in front of them, all facing one behind the other, toward the west. Jake followed the body with the voice into a bunker that appeared to be half cut into the ridge base and half made of wood. Tubman and two soldiers were behind him. They passed small rooms with half-opened doors that were crowded with men at radios and telephones—or so Jake thought. Soldiers in the narrow hallway looked at Jake without expression. The smell of sweat and cigarette smoke seemed to be the composition of the air. Jake thought, shit. Oh, shit.

They arrived at a door. The soldier with the voice—he did not wear rank—knocked and, without waiting, opened it.

Obika looked up, not suddenly, but with the air of one for whom there are no more surprises. The Pandemis saluted. Jake saluted; he thought Obika looked exhausted, yet something danced with slow grace in his eyes.

Tubman wheeled around the desk that was almost bare, and bent to whisper in Obika's ear—Obika, who had not stopped looking at Jake since the moment they entered. For one second Obika's eyes flickered to Jake's bag, then back to Jake's face. He nodded impatiently. "Out," he said, flicking his fingers at Tubman, the soldier with the voice and the two with the rifles. M-1 carbines, Jake saw. The Pandemi soldiers saluted. Obika returned the salute with the energy of a second lieutenant passing through a company in basic training.

When the door closed behind them, Obika said, "Well, Major, you've come."

Jake was puzzled. Still at attention, he said, "Wasn't I invited, General?"

Obika bent his head in a clumsy, exhausted gesture of graciousness. "Of course."

The pitch of the wind hit the ridge like a blow, a dull, long, *thooom*, and driving rain began to hammer the ceiling and the ground outside like bullets from an unheard plane.

"Sit down, Major."

Jake sat, dropping the bag beside him, wondering if they knew or merely guessed what was in it.

"We don't have much time, so let me get right to the point, the way you Americans like to, I've heard. We *did* have an appointment, but until the call came from the North Gate, I didn't believe you were really coming." Obika glanced at the map of Pandemi on the wall. "Even with Tubman escorting."

Jake dug into his shirt pocket. "May I smoke, sir?"

Obika's smile was wan. "Sure. But do you understand what I'm saying?"

Jake lighted and exhaled. "No, sir."

Obika sighed and raised his eyes to the ceiling as though to see the rain. "It's simple. We know you came to help—what is it you Americans say? Take out the reactor"—he broke off to raise both hands to ward off Jake's protest—"we *know*. To what extent *you* were involved we did not know until Tubman came in with you. Then our information fell somewhat into place."

Jake tried to roll his eyes, to communicate exasperation, but his eyes resisted; they remained fixed on Obika's full, smooth-skinned face.

Obika spoke in cadenced tones. "They have dealt you out, Major Henry. Had you been in, Klein would not have let you come at this particular time."

Jake ran his finger down the side of his nose and looked at the slight sheen of oil on his forefinger.

"You've been on the road a few hours, so let me tell you what's occurring. President Fasseke's chief of staff has been murdered. Lieutenant Mbunde—you met him—killed him with help from soldiers now in his command. They have taken over Bagui—"

"Chuma?" Jake interrupted. "Chuma?"

"The president is safe, Major. But the police have gone over to Mbunde. How could they not? Klein's offers were most generous."

Jake felt relief that Fasseke was all right; he also felt relief that at this point at least Obika did not consider him a part of the plot. Right, Jake thought. He wasn't. That cocksucker Klein. The sonofabitch. I have been, Jake realized, a goddamn decoy all along.

Obika continued. "Mbunde has taken the radio station, but hasn't yet announced the coup. He'll finish up tonight. If he doesn't, daylight'll be another story. They always do these at night."

"You seem to have all the information you need, General," Jake said.

"Yes, communication is busy, but we don't know for how long. The Chinese and Soviet embassies are under attack. They're keeping us informed—but they're destroying files, they say, so . . ."

Jake drew hard on his cigarette. His throat stung. Somewhere he began to tremble, like a man having charges read to him. "Your troops in the south?" he asked. His voice sounded unnatural.

"The Bacle Barracks went to Mbunde. *Mbunde!*" Obika said. "Can it be possible that Pandemi will be run by Mbunde? Christ!"

Jake looked for an ashtray. Obika shoved him one across his desktop. "You ought to be able to handle him, General."

"Maybe. After Jija Deep, Major. We're ready to go there now." Obika stood and placed his hand on the yellowed map of Pandemi.

211

"Our radar," he said, "President Shaguri's radar, shows some activity along the Ulcuma coast. Here." Obika thumped a thick black finger on the map. "Those firefights you heard are your diversion, designed to keep us here rather than in Jija Deep. We didn't bite; we're playing it out. I expect the wind and rain are making it difficult for your men to keep on whatever schedule they have. We're moving out soon. We can't wait for the Temian troops to join us. Probably caught in the weather too." Obika turned away from the map. "I don't suppose you know how many Americans or whoever, are coming, do you?"

"No, sir." Jake stared at the plank flooring.

Obika began to shuffle back and forth behind his desk. He glanced at his watch. "Your sergeant should be here shortly. What do you want to do with him?"

Jake searched Obika's face. "I don't understand, sir."

"You must have suspected he was to do you harm, Major."

"It crossed my mind, but I don't know why."

Obika stopped shuffling. "He was going to kill you, Major. That's our information. That they were going to plant your body inside Ulcuma. You can imagine the complications, the publicity resulting from that. It would make your Senator Ellender look good."

Ellender had visited Africa and proclaimed that Africans and Afro-Americans had nothing whatsoever in common.

Obika sat down on the edge of his chair. "You were to be a pawn, Major Henry. Look, let me tell you: ever since President Fasseke took office, your people have been covered by houseboys and whores, market people, hotel help, gas station attendants; janitors, secretaries, receptionists. Not that the

212

embassy didn't screen the people they hired, but we have been here for a long, long time. We let them believe we didn't know how to bug rooms, tap phones, take photos. It's all easy because the Americans try to keep to themselves. They buy boats, have their own beach, go to the same restaurants, fuck one another's wives or each other, I don't know which, or care. We knew who you were by the time you and that sergeant arrived in Bagui. We just weren't sure where you fitted in. Now. What do you want to do with the sergeant?''

Jake said nothing.

Obika laughed in his chest without opening his mouth. "Well, then, he'll have to take your place, won't he? Except he'll be found at Jija."

"And me?"

"What, kill you? No, no. President Fasseke wouldn't hear of it. He's a man whose loyalties run deep and long. Besides, you will be doing him a very great favor—" Obika rose. "The sergeant is here, Major."

Jake hadn't heard anything through the rain sounds; he looked at Obika with new appreciation.

The soldier without rank came in, walked quickly to Obika and began to whisper into his ear. Obika nodded. "Tell the sergeant this: Major Henry left orders for him to proceed to the Ulcuma frontier, where he will find Major Henry observing." Obika looked directly at Jake. "Ten minutes drive from here, kill him. Shoot him in the front, the front. Then bring his body back here and put it on the rear truck. With the radio, is that clear, with the radio."

"Yes, sir." The soldier left without saluting.

Jake lit another cigarette. He and Obika looked at each

other. Obika shrugged. "War is hell," he said, and smiled. "We thought to leave the Uzi with him too. That's what you have, Major? But you may need that."

"For what?" Jake's voice was flat, dry. He pumped cigarette ash into the ashtray.

"You and Tubman are going to Temian. With a very special passenger who should be arriving very soon."

"Busy place," Jake said. "Who's the passenger, and what do I do after I get to Temian?"

"Your car's gassed up. No one will shoot at an American official. You'll get back to Bagui safe enough. Your friend Klein won't be expecting you. Go home. Look up Ouro. You met him. Find his friend, that black American writer. Tell them: write our story. Keep writing it, and someday it'll all come out."

"The passenger?" Jake said.

"Mrs. Fasseke." Obika watched Jake grind out his cigarette. "You see, I am demanding some loyalty from you in return, Major. Tubman—he's a mean one, you know, but he's a good and loyal soldier—will pose as your civilian driver." Obika turned to the map again. "You'll go by the east road. Captain Tubman knows the way."

Obika saw that the American, like a soldier in his first action, was frozen. He looked down at his hands, cupped one inside the other, stared at his knuckles, at his fingernails. They needed cleaning. "Major, are you all right?"

"Yes, sir."

"Good. This is a different kind of war. I suspect that Vietnam will be a different kind of war for you Americans; the French found it so. But you must understand that this is the kind of war you'll be fighting for a long, long time, Major

Henry, unless, of course, you and the Soviets decide to see just what your nukes will do."

"Jija Deep," Jake heard himself say. "What happens there?"

"You'll destroy it and kill my men and maybe me in the process, but it's being shut down. The order came while you were on the road." Obika paused. "I understand that everything necessary to prevent a mishap has been done or is being done."

Jake nodded. He was glad he would be going the other way. He saw Obika's gaze dart to the door.

"I think your passenger's here. You might as well take the gun out of the bag. Keep it handy. Ah, yes, Major Henry." Obika came from behind the desk and planted himself face-to-face with Jake. "Mrs. Fasseke is pregnant." Jake felt Obika's breath upon his face. "This morning she found out. The president doesn't yet know."

The door opened and the soldier without rank entered once more. "Ready, sir. The car and the trucks."

"The Temian troops?"

"No word at all, sir."

Obika returned to his desk, opened a drawer, and took out a .45 with pearl handles that was strapped to a belt. He grinned at Jake. "A gift from your Captain Gilchrist."

"Patton," Jake said. He wanted another cigarette.

"Yes, Patton," Obika said, strapping on. "They never say in your battle histories anything about the black tankers, do they?"

Jake remained silent. He didn't know anything about black World War Two tankers either. Tubman entered. Through the open door Jake could hear engines running and the rain still driving down. The place seemed to be emptying out. Jake wanted to ask the soldier without rank if he had killed Coates, if Coates's body was in the rear truck with bullet holes in the front.

Obika pulled on a cap and then shook hands with Tubman and the other soldier; they saluted. Obika shook hands with Jake.

"Between you and Tubman, you should accomplish your mission in good form. Good luck, Major Henry."

Jake saluted and murmured, "Yes, sir. Thanks. Good luck to you, sir."

Obika vanished in the darkness outside. The lights had been cut. The soldier followed him, resting his hand momentarily in Tubman's. "Luck," the soldier said.

"Luck to you too," Tubman answered. He turned to Jake. "Ready, Major?" He formed a grin. "Don't I look just like a regular Pandemi houseboy?" The grin vanished as quickly as it had appeared. Tubman stood aside as Jake passed out. Tubman pressed out the light. "Your car's over there. Follow me," Tubman said.

Bent against the rain, they slithered through the muddy road toward the eerie glow of the parking lights of the car. Behind him Jake saw an endless line of slowly moving, dull red taillights. He thought about Coates as darkness and trees swallowed the last red pair of lights.

Jake held the Uzi and his bag with one hand as he entered the back of the car while Tubman slipped into the front. Jake smelled the perfume—light, innocent—before he could make out her form.

"Mrs. Fasseke, this is Major Henry, the president's childhood friend. Don't worry about the gun. He's on our side."

FOURTEEN

The rain forests were weeping and the branches of the trees were snapping and swinging in the heavy winds; the rains beat the petals of flowers off their limbs and onto the ground; the red earth in darkness was wounded and bleeding, the red water at first pounding into the ridge above the plant, into the beach beyond the neck, and then the earth gave up, opened itself to receive and absorb the rain.

Inside the plant the control rods had been fixed in the fuel rods. The rate of water coolant had been upped to 3.1 million gallons per minute, and the engineers were grateful that full power had not been achieved during the short time the plant was functioning. Hot water was still boiling from the outlet pipes; steam rose from the inlet. The engineers knew that soldiers had taken up positions near the pumps, the steam generator, the intake and outlet pipes; they were on the ridge and covering the neck through which the sea thundered, sending waves spraying like flocks of bombs at the inside of the neck. The water temperature inside the reactor was dropping, was now at 225 degrees Fahrenheit, and the engineers were beginning to breathe easier.

They heard the wind fly down the ridge and buffet the buildings, and then the rain stopped. Outside, the stars began to appear in the eastern sky, as though a giant hand were sweeping away the clouds, shoving them disdainfully toward the west.

That was when, inside the quieting plant, the engineers heard the first shots. Those who had windows in their stations ran to them in time to see flares popping daylight over Jija Deep. There came louder explosions and the engineers could tell which station was under attack; the engineers checked their monitors and waited. They did not really look at each other as the sounds grew louder and closer; they watched the monitors. One or two nodded to no one in particular, nods that indicated that all was going to be all right as far as anyone knew inside the plant. Buzzers and phones no longer worked; each station was on its own, each engineer alone at his post watching monitors and adjusting gauges, pushing this or that button, following the direction of indicators away from red to deep into green.

Yema Fasseke sat with her neck against the back of the car seat, her head tilted toward the roof, her eyes closing and opening. She opened her window to get fresh air; both the American and Tubman were chain-smoking.

Before them, just cresting a hill, came a convoy of trucks, their bodies and tires thick with red mud. Tubman pulled to the side. "Temians, I hope they're not too late," he said into the first light of day. He lowered his window and pumped his arm. "Hurry, hurry!" he shouted.

Jake could see that the soldiers were tired. Their fatigues were covered with drying red mud, even their hands with which they loosely held their rifles. Their eyes were red; they were sitting slackly on the bases of their spines. Jake remembered seeing troops, American troops, looking just like that in winter sixteen years before in Korea. But those troops had been bloodied and were in retreat; these had not yet arrived at the fire zone. Tubman, Jake thought, must have seen it too. He was pumping his arm and shouting in a dialect, an exhortation (what else) Jake imagined. The passing soldiers looked down with glazed, exhausted eyes which rested, just briefly, on the flags that were still drying. The trucks groaned past. "Temians!" Tubman hissed.

He pulled back on the road. Jake leaned on the top of the front seat. He wished Tubman would find the window spray and clean the windshield. Now the sun began to lighten the sky ahead of them and its heat forced up soft, billowing levels of steam through which the sun's rays shone. The gas tank was half empty.

"Got more gas?" Jake asked.

Tubman nodded and jerked his thumb backward. "In the trunk."

Jake leaned back. "Tired?" he asked Yema Fasseke.

She had a strong, full face, slightly slanted eyes, carefully carved lips, and long lashes. She smiled. "I am fine, Major."

"Good." He smiled. "Whoops!" The car had skidded again in a pocket of mud. "We'd make better time if we had a jeep, Tubman," he said.

"Our jeeps don't have American flags flying from them, Major. This is better for Mrs. Fasseke anyway."

"I don't think I'll break in two, Captain."

"No, missus, but the car is safer."

"I understand." She turned to Jake. "So, it happened that you never did come for dinner, Major."

"No, I didn't. I'm sorry."

"Another time," she said.

"Yes," Jake said. He glanced up and saw Tubman looking at him.

Tubman said, "Another time? Yes, let's hope so."

"Do you want me to take a turn, Captain?"

"I'd love to, but we just don't know who's going to pop out of the bush, do we? It looks better this way. I'm all right. I'm out of cigarettes though."

Jake fished in his bag and found a pack. He opened it and lit a cigarette for Tubman and passed it over. He lay the pack on the seat beside him.

Tubman inhaled deeply and eased the smoke out of his mouth and nostrils. "Thanks."

"How much longer, Captain?" Mrs. Fasseke asked.

"At this rate, missus, about two hours. Can't go any faster. I wish we could, though, before things dry out. Then we'll leave a trail of dust, and I don't want President Shaguri's pilots to make a mistake. Even if the lines were open, we wouldn't have called. Too dangerous."

"Yes, I see. It's all right, Captain. Please don't worry on my account."

Jake cradled the Uzi muzzle away from Mrs. Fasseke. His eyelids sank; he forced them open. They sank again.

"Major!" Tubman shouted. "Keep awake!"

"I'm okay, I'm okay," Jake said. He turned to Yema Fasseke.

"Which are you hoping for, boy or girl?"

"Boy, of course."

"For Chuma?"

"Yes. And for me."

Jake saw Tubman in the rearview mirror. Tubman winked. He said, "I never had time to get married, missus."

"Like General Obika, yes? The army is your wife. But the major is married."

"They have time for such things in the American army, missus. Here we are real soldiers."

"Which means," Jake said, feeling himself climb out of his weariness, "you've probably been married three times."

Tubman laughed for the first time. "Even if I could afford three wives, I wouldn't want them. Too much work."

They bantered as they rode through the rising steam until there was steam no more. Once they stopped so Yema Fasseke could vanish in the forest for a few moments. Jake showed Tubman the spray and they cleaned the windows, then filled the tank from the gas can. Jake adjusted the air conditioner. They drank from Tubman's canteen when Yema Fasseke returned. Jake drew one more breath of the wet-smelling forest, now beginning to simmer with heat. They climbed inside and started off again.

An hour later they began to climb toward the plateau that signaled the beginning of the end of Pandemi territory. Tubman's eyes kept shooting toward the rearview mirror.

Jake turned but could see nothing. "What is it?"

"I don't know. I saw something flash in the sun a couple of times."

"Can we speed up?"

"We don't know who's on our side of the border crossing, Major, ours or Mbunde's. We're too close to get foolhardy."

Tubman swung carefully off the road, finding spaces between trees and mounds, and eased through the grasses until they faced the road once again. He killed the engine. Jake got out and crept to the side of the road. He heard the grasses swish; Tubman slid down beside him and pressed his ear to the ground. He looked up at Jake with a grin and said, "Yes." He took out his pistol.

The grasses were still damp, but the wet felt good in the heat. There were birdsounds and windsounds and then a clanking, labored sound of old metal, a barrel sent rolling along the road, Jake thought. They lay still, waiting. Jake was sorry they hadn't found a better vantage point, so they would not have to make a decision, any decision, until the last moment. Like wayward shutters, the grasses bent in the breeze before them. The sound grew louder. Jake flicked off the safety, aimed at the sound, which was now upon them. Jake had one small angle through which he saw, before the vehicle was abreast of them, a spattered and dented crimson, lime, and gold-colored bus. "Wait!" he whispered to Tubman. "Hold it. Give me cover, but hold it." Jake rose up with his legs, slowly, straight up so that he became a part of the terrain.

Mr. Fasseke was leaning against the door; he seemed asleep. The other person seemed to be holding the steering wheel in desperation; his face was laced with strain. Uncle Bonaco.

"Mr. Fasseke! Uncle Bonaco!"

Tubman leaped up. "Who?"

Mr. Fasseke awoke with a start and a jolt in the side from Uncle Bonaco. Jake waved his arms. "It's me, Jacob. Stop!" He saw Mr. Fasseke's eyes travel upward, swiftly, to the hand in which Jake was holding the Uzi; he said something quickly to his brother, and the old bus whined as Bonaco tried to give it gas, but the bus squatted and popped and shuddered and moved on at the same rate of speed.

Tubman leaped up, shouting in dialect, running to and beside the bus. His voice cracked against the brightness of the morning. Jake heard the grasses hissing behind him and turned, lowering the gun to his hip. Mrs. Fasseke. But Mr. Fasseke had seen her before Jake, and turned once again to his brother. The bus slowed and stopped. Mr. Fasseke, half-jumping, half-falling, came out of the bus with a tire iron in his hand. Tubman laughed, fell down laughing. Yema Fasseke shouted once she took in the scene. "Father Akenzua! Father!" And now Bonaco lumbered out on his side, clutching a thick stick. "It's all right, Father, it's all right." She embraced Mr. Fasseke, who still glowered at Jake and Tubman, who was climbing to his feet again, holstering his pistol.

They gathered in the shade of a tree, were there when two Blue Squadron jets howled out of the east and strafed the bus in two passes. Akenzua and Bonaco said nothing. The bus was ruined. The planes, the sound of their screams diminishing into a high-pitched hum, vanished back into the rising sunlight. There was an eerie silence as Akenzua and Bonaco went to the bus and gathered their shredded belongings. Yema Fasseke hovered near, as though she could ward off more bad luck. The three moved through the grasses in the bright sunlight as if in pantomime. Tubman peered at them from beneath his slightly lowered head. Jake wanted to help, but felt a stranger in a ritual who did not know the rules, and so he watched them; he opened the car trunk and watched them throw in the shreds of plastic bags and shirts and pants. Then he moved to check the fastenings on the flags. The flags themselves were dry; they whipped and cracked bravely in the slight, hot wind.

Once in the car, Yema Fasseke sandwiched between Jake and Akenzua, Bonaco in front with Tubman, the air began to quiver with dialect. Yema Fasseke spoke in soothing tones, but there seemed to be questions directed at Tubman by Akenzua and Bonaco, and looks that burned, cut, and stung were unleashed in Jake's direction. Jake drew up within himself, the way he did when whites around him directed their conversations only to one another.

They no longer skidded, for the road was drying fast, even sending out puffs of dust now and again. For now the windows were open; shut the riders seemed pressed too tightly together. Jake's eyes began to close once more; he forced them open, wondering how Tubman managed. Surely Tubman was not a better soldier than he.

Finally, Akenzua spoke. "Jacob," he said. "The soldier has been telling us of your bravery, of your willingness to help my daughter-in-law escape Pandemi to join my son."

Jake glanced at Tubman; Tubman looked back in the mirror. There was no expression on his face.

"Our thanks," Akenzua said. Bonaco nodded as though to agree.

Jake looked from Akenzua to Bonaco to Tubman.

"We are glad it turned out that you were on our side after all," Uncle Bonaco said.

224

"Yes," Akenzua said.

"How do you happen to be on this road, Mr. Fasseke?" Jake asked.

Akenzua shrugged. "We didn't even know what was going on. We were going to Jija Near, and soldiers kept sending us off this way, this way, until we were in the camp when we learned. They wouldn't let us return south for Yema. They told us they thought Chuma was in Temian. When we found out where this road was headed, we just kept going."

"They don't know anything about anything," Tubman said. "Just like us. Pity you don't have a radio in this car, Major."

"I'm glad you and Uncle Bonaco and Mrs. Fasseke are all right," Jake said. He was feeling alternately heavy with the need to sleep and light-headed because he hadn't.

"Major," Tubman said. "Are you all right? The border should be coming up in a few minutes. Everybody on his toes. Major?"

"Stop," Jake said. "Stop and get off the road."

Tubman maintained his speed. Jake felt the glances of Akenzua, Bonaco, and Yema Fasseke, and another silence filled the car. Finally, Tubman lifted his chin and nodded his head; he slowed, found a place to get off the road, and drove carefully into the high grasses and bush.

"Why, Jacob? Why soldier? Why do you do this?" Akenzua demanded.

Tubman turned off the motor and left the key in the ignition. "The major's right," he said. "We'll go check the crossing. If it's all right with our people, we'll come back. If we have trouble and *don't* come back, then you'll have to drive until you find another route, a cattle track, a footpath, anything that'll take you into Temian. Ready, Major?"

Jake climbed out. "Ready."

"I'll take the other side," Tubman said, and he scooted across the road. Jake, crouching, kept even with him, moved slowly through the grasses. He glanced behind; the car was already invisible. Every few steps he raised clear to check Tubman's progress. Jake sweated. Insects buzzed around him, bit him. A horde of tiny silverflies hovered above him. He began to smell himself. Sweat dripped from his nose, ran down the contours of his face. He pushed aside limbs with the Uzi. Out of the corner of his eye he saw Tubman wave, his hand just barely clearing the grasses. Tubman seemed to be patting his hand against the air. He stopped and sank again into the grasses. Jake leaned against a small tree, grateful for its shade; he could see the place where Tubman stopped. He was human after all; got tired like anyone else. He wondered why Tubman had made him a hero. The guy knew he didn't have any choice. It was carry Yema Fasseke to Temian or wind up like Coates; no secret about that; didn't even have to ask about that one. Jake strained to see Tubman's spot; it looked the way it must have looked for years—empty. Good soldier, Jake thought. In the field, not driving through army camps. Maybe he had his orders, but, hell. Jake heard a bird. He thought it was a bird whose cry, he realized, seemed unusual. He hadn't realized that he had already internalized the different birdsounds. He glanced across the road again and saw Tubman's hand; this time an index finger pointed forward. Jake began to move again.

It took a half hour before they gained a view of the crossing with its makeshift barrier, painted red and white, placed low upon two pieces of wood across the road on the Temain side.

The barrier on the Pandemi side and the guardpost were unmanned. There were two soldiers on the Temian side. Tubman raised the birdcall again and they withdrew, moving with more speed and less caution back to the car, where they emptied Tubman's canteen.

It would have been faster if Jake or Tubman had alerted the guards to their coming. But any soldier with good sense would have had reservations. No, the car with the American flags flying would do the job, and quite properly.

The soldiers were asleep when they rumbled up to the barrier and stopped. Tubman blew the horn. The soldiers started and with rifles at the ready approached the car. Jake got out, the muzzle of the Uzi pointing downward. The soldiers stared at him, puzzled. Tubman leaned his head out of the window and spoke in dialect. The soldiers saluted Jake and Jake returned crisply.

"Water, and have them call somebody," Jake told Tubman.

Tubman spoke sharply, pointing at Yema Fasseke, to her father-in-law and Bonaco. The soldiers bowed, rushed to their guardpost, and returned with canteens of water. They pointed to the shade of a giant ebony tree. "There you rest," they said to Yema Fasseke.

Jake watched her; Akenzua and Bonaco trudged wearily to the split-log benches beneath the tree. He and Tubman went with the soldiers to the guardpost. "What's happened, did they say?" Jake asked.

"Bad," Tubman said. "Mbunde's got it all."

"Jija Deep, General Obika?"

"They don't know."

"So what do you do?" Jake asked.

"Stay in Temian until we take it back."

Jake nodded. His weariness made him crouch before he fell. "Why did you tell them that business about Mrs. Fasseke?"

Tubman shrugged. "Why not? It was easier than explaining everything to them, wasn't it?"

They paused to listen to one soldier talking on the phone. He was grinning. "Fasseke," he said, "President Fasseke. In Accara. Accara!"

"Did you know that?" Jake asked Tubman.

"No, but I guessed that's where he would be."

Akenzua came running in a slow, slew-footed gait.

"The president is in Accara," Tubman said. "He's all right."

Akenzua went back to his daughter-in-law at a quicker pace. Jake tried not to look as she sank her face into her knees and sobbed.

Jake walked in small squares. Being in a crouch was work. Tubman watched him with a sardonic smile. "Major, you do all right. Do you suppose your armies could win a war in this part of Africa?"

Jake stopped. "Okay. I came along for the ride. Listen, captain, *nobody* can win a war in this part of Africa."

Tubman grinned. "I'll bet you you lose in Vietnam. You lost in Korea, didn't you? And that wasn't even in the tropics." Tubman shook his head.

"Why would we have to fight a war in Africa, Captain?"

"For the same reason you think you have to fight a war in Vietnam."

Jake stopped marching. The Temian soldiers danced toward them. Whatever they had to say they were saying to

Tubman in dialect. Tubman was nodding in jerks as though to say "Yes?" "Yes." Then he pointed to Yema Fasseke, Akenzua, and Bonaco, and the soldiers danced away.

"What'd they say?" Jake asked. He was tired of asking the question. It was somehow unreal, this business of black people being unable to communicate with one another in a common tongue.

"They're sending a helicopter for us. What do you want to do, Major?"

"What General Obika wanted me to do. Drive back to Bagui."

"There'll be problems, I take it—"

"What do you mean?"

"All I know is that you're a spy. I ran over a Pandemi soldier to maintain a certain speed so you wouldn't jump out. The general wanted to see you at once. So, Major, you have problems because you have a missing driver."

Jake paced this time instead of marching; Tubman kept step with him. "No problem, Captain. They don't expect me to return. The element of surprise. Surprise, remember? And I'll be flying the flag. How long a drive is it, and is there more gas?"

"More gas," Tubman said, "in that can. But you'd better take these too." He dug into his pocket and brought out a handful of kola nuts. "Suck them, don't chew."

Jake accepted them. "Kola nuts?"

"Yes. Why don't you get some rest before they come for us?"

Jake turned the nuts over with his thumb. "I need directions."

"Okay. I can get them. Let you know when you wake."

Jake moved to the shade, where Akenzua patted down a place next to him. "Rest, Jacob," Akenzua said, "Rest."

The helicopter came in fast, low, and dark over the ragged treeline, and Jake awoke with a start and sat bolt upright; for a moment he was cold as hell and was in Korea. Then he saw the craft settling down, smashing grasses and bulleting dust. Tubman was already helping Mrs. Fasseke up, Jake saw through the red, stinging cloud; Akenzua and Bonaco, their eyes fixed distrustfully on the helicopter, were climbing, scrambling to their feet, where they stood, protecting their faces with their arms. Still struggling to return to his center, from fright to understanding, Jake recognized old Africa and new Africa in the noisy portrait of the two men and the helicopter.

Jake did not understand the hurry; the pilot was signaling, *come on, come on, get in, get in.* Whatever was done was done. Instinctively he looked around for the car and saw that it had been more or less wiped clean of dust and mud; smeared, it looked better than it had.

They stood bunched up cowering under the whirling blades; they were looking at him; he jogged toward them. This was good-bye? In thunder and dust? It seemed he had been with them forever.

Yema Fasseke embraced him, kissed his cheek; Akenzua seized him on one side, and Bonaco on the other. Jake could not hear their voices; he could not hear his own: "Good luck! Good luck!"

Akenzua was shouting, but Jake could not hear; he grasped the man's hand and yelled, "I hope Uncle Bonaco gets another bus!" but Uncle Bonaco was already offering a feeble grin, the way people do when they cannot hear.

Tubman hefted his hand toward Jake and as Jake took it, Tubman leaned to his ear. "There's a map in the car. Good luck! Fuck the U.S.!" He climbed in; the pilot had already seated and belted in the others. Tubman was waving him away; his mouth was moving exaggeratedly: *Stand clear! Stand clear!* Jake read. His head lowered, Jake ran from beneath the blades; they were moving faster now. The craft thundered up at a tilt, bruising the grasses once more, spewing dust in a thicker cloud; it lumbered over the treetops, its hammering growing softer and softer until Jake could hear it no longer. He was alone with the soldiers and they were looking at him.

Jake pointed to himself. "I go now." He made a pushing motion with the skin side of his hand. "Which way? Road?"

"Road," one of the soldiers said with a triumphant grin. He pointed down the narrow track that led to the guardpost; his finger went up and down, and then he moved his arm to the right and repeated the motions. Jake nodded and broke off to get the map from the car. He showed it to the soldiers and they peered at it and nodded at Tubman's arrows, Jake's skin-cracked finger. They stood near when Jake got in the car to check the gas gauge and the water left in Tubman's canteen. Satisfied, he held out his hand and they each shook it and saluted. Jake whipped one off in return, but it all seemed foolish there in the silence that was not quite still. He eased the car down the road and remembered the stripped kola nuts. He dug two out of his pocket and began to suck on them. He was alone, he thought, for the first time (except for being in bed) since his return to Africa.

It was late, dark, when he let himself into the flat and pressed the light switch. The flags and his papers had gotten him through the several cordons into and within the city, where a curfew had been imposed. Jake didn't know if he was hungrier than sleepy. He smelled nothing that had been cooked. But it was Sunday night, not Sunday morning, he remembered.

He dropped his bag with a dull and muffled clank to the floor, turned on the radio, and went to the kitchen; there he took from the refrigerator the bottle of water that rested almost alone on a shelf. He brought that and the Scotch back to the room with the radio. He gulped directly from the whiskey; he didn't recall that so much of it was gone. Then he took a long, luxurious drink, was drinking when he realized no sound was coming from the radio save a slight hiss. He adjusted dials; no sound. Nothing. Off the air? He thought of the phone, turned to look at it. No. Not now. He was feeling warm and woozy.

Shower, he thought, but he went to the balcony and looked up and down the silent street. Another drink. He took off the pistol belt and threw it on his bed; he stripped and entered the shower, but not before he took what was left of the Scotch and another drink of water. Mosquitoes hummed; the smell of dried plaster, sweet, pungent, hung in the bathroom. Jake tested the water; it was warm, the spray soft and fat. He stepped in and sighed aloud and let the water drum upon his head, his shoulders, his back. He stroked himself with soap and continued to sigh, and he felt sleep lurching toward him.

He turned off the water and reached for a towel; his fingers had just caressed its damp folds when it seemed to jerk into his hand.

"Hello, Major."

Dawson. Jake took the towel and wrapped it around his waist.

"Tired? Hungry?"

"Sleepy," Jake said. Why was it that Dawson didn't sound like himself?

"I can fix you something if you like."

"No. Fix the radio."

"They're not broadcasting at this hour, Major."

Dawson stood aside to let Jake pass, accompanied by a cloud of steam. "You drink my Scotch?"

"There's more. Shall I get it?"

"Yeah. Please." Jake stood in the living room, drying himself, digging deep between his legs, massaging his face; he started to feel the coolness that always came momentarily right after he'd bathed.

Dawson returned with two glasses, both half-filled. Dawson sat down. "How was the trip?"

"Okay." Jake was looking toward the balcony, but flicking his eyes back to Dawson.

"Good," Dawson said. "I see you didn't have to use the Uzi."

Jake sat down and turned directly toward Dawson, waiting.

Dawson sipped. "Good thing. Doesn't work."

Jake glared at Dawson, then dropped his eyes to see how much of his drink remained. "You knew about Coates?"

"We guessed about Coates and we thought you were not

important in all this, so why not throw a favor your way? Of course, we didn't know anything for *sure*. Only the way white people usually are."

"President Fasseke *is* all right?"

"Quite all right."

Jake grinned out of his weariness which the Scotch was rapidly overtaking. "You speak very good English now Dawson."

Dawson said nothing.

"So, now what?" Jake asked.

"We'll get it back. Some of us are still in place."

Jake said, "So I see. What happened to the plant?"

"They took it out, but it didn't go anywhere near critical. Klein is dancing in his sleep. He's expecting Coates, not you. But he's worried that he hasn't heard from your driver." Here Dawson smiled.

"Coates," Jake said, "*is* dead?"

Dawson swept up the bottle that was behind his chair. He inclined it toward Jake. Jake held out his glass and watched the liquid flow into it. Dawson helped himself. He set the bottle on the floor. "Yes, and four others. Mercenaries, I think you call them."

"Obika?"

"Guinea."

Jake held his lips wide and drank. "Anything flying out of here?"

Dawson leaned forward. "You leaving, Major?" He smiled.

"If you were Klein, what would you do with me?"

Dawson said, nodding, "Get you the hell out of here. Or kill you. But since he's not managed to do that or have that done, fly you home or somewhere else." Dawson paused. "Paris, maybe?"

Jake stood. "I'm going to bed. No phone calls, please."

Dawson gave a short laugh. "What time you want to get up to see Klein?"

"Want to run out the string, huh?"

"Why not, Major?"

"Nine. And listen, man. You've done such a good job of faking everyone out, why don't you pack my bags, too, and have them ready?"

"All right. There is a plane due in at noon. Through Paris. Want me to take care of it?"

"No," Jake mumbled. "Klein will want to take care of it."

Dawson stood and finished his drink in a gulp. "Nine then."

Jake closed the door after him, slipping on the lock which he now knew was useless because Dawson had the key and, maybe, a few other people as well. In his bedroom Jake took out the Uzi and pulled out the magazine. He studied the gun carefully, but could see nothing wrong with it. He pulled the trigger as hard as he could and it fell clattering to the floor. It had been mostly filed through. Jake threw the gun into a chair. "Shit!"

F I F T E E N

. 🦅 .

Bagui didn't look like a city under seige, but, Jake Henry thought, he didn't *know* how a city in that state was supposed to look or how its inhabitants were supposed to react. *Pictures* he'd seen, the most recent those of Seventh Avenue in Harlem and 103rd Street, Watts, in Los Angeles; but those were not cities, only sections of them; the rest of New York and Los Angeles had pretty much gone on about their business. Why should it be different here? But there was a difference, Dawson had told him over breakfast in his perfect English. There had not been a single death in the entire country. Dawson had caught himself and amended his statement. "Maybe three or four. Or five or six, but none that most people will ever know about."

Bathed in bright sunlight, people walked or biked through the streets as though nothing at all had happened, pausing only to turn at the sounds of cars rushing up behind them. The road blocks of last night were gone, those cordons that made even the coolest heartbeat kick to a higher rhythm. There were more police around than Jake remembered, and the occasional jeep filled with soldiers who saluted Jake's flags, gave him some pause. But a newcomer would not have seen any degree of change, for the change was slight.

Jake passed a creaking bus that was filled with yammering Pandemis, and he thought of Uncle Bonaco, of Mr. Fasseke, and Chuma and his wife. So near home and yet, across the border because of the coup, so far away. It was true that some of Fasseke's people were "still in place," as Dawson had put it, but Chuma's enemy was not Mbunde; it was America. Mbunde, Jake thought, like me, is only a tool.

The Chinese and Soviet embassies were ringed by police and soldiers. Jake wondered why. It had been Jake's impression that no one took the jive connections Pandemi had with the Russians and the Chinese seriously. There was not a single African nation to which the Chinese and Russians had shown full commitment so far; they were like Americans feeling their way along the corridors in a dark place.

Of course, he could always ask Klein why the Soviets and Chinese were so heavily protected, but he had every reason not to expect the truth in any shape, form, or fashion, not now, definitely not now. He and Klein had recognized each other instantly, Jake recalled. Hatred at first sight; he'd had the experience before. Commanders at all levels of the army were not unknown to have had squads, platoons, companies, and even larger units annihilated to have a single man they may have disliked killed. In action. The phrase carried the cover of honor against which no one could argue.

Spies, on the other hand, simply vanished, as he would have had it not been for the Dawsons, the Tubmans, the Obikas, and Chuma, who had predicated their moves on an internalized knowledge of the Western psyche and at the end gave him, Jake, an option not usually made available to Westerners, his compatriots. They had pitied him, even Tubman, who could smash his own trooper without a backward glance, and so had Obika who, about to enter the eye of the storm, could save his, Jake's life, and take Coates's in return. This morning, driving slowly toward the embassy of the United States, that seemed eminently fair.

I came into this place like the coolest lion, Jake thought, and leave it like a leper, despised by some, pitied by others, and unknown by most. In under a week, a goddam week.

"There are some people," Dawson had said to him when he left, "who are like birds. Birds have no mirrors. They do not know what they look like, only what they can do. Set up a glass wall and they'll fly into it seeking the prey they see there. They break their necks and they die."

Jake pulled up at the embassy motor pool. The embassy, too, was well covered, backed up by marines in fatigues and in helmets and gun belts. He left his luggage in the car. "I'm going to need a driver," he told the sergeant in charge, "when I come back. Airport."

"The Joberg–Paris flight, sir?"

"You got it."

"Right."

"Wasn't Coates with you, sir, when you checked out?"

"Coates got himself another assignment, Sergeant."

The embassy was quiet; even the library, run by the USIS

across the street, appeared empty. Jake walked quickly to the travel section, rested his papers momentarily before the clerk, and said, "Please cut me some travel orders for that KLM noon flight to Paris. Open ticket from Paris to New York on anything."

"Henry," the clerk mumbled. "Henry." Then he whipped around a corner and returned with a great smile. "They were cut by Mr. Klein not an hour ago."

Jake checked the tickets. "No. this is Dakar–New York. I want Paris and then New York."

The clerk hesitated. "Do it," Jake said. "I'll be back in fifteen minutes."

They must have seen the car, Jake thought, and maybe he doesn't want to know anything about Coates. He would have checked and found him absent. Jake wondered if Travel was speaking to Klein right at this moment.

Jake traversed the halls without speaking to anyone. What was there to say? He opened Klein's door without knocking and closed it behind him. Klein was sitting; his tennis shirt looked damp and tired. Although his face was sagging and puffed, his eyes were alert; they darted up, blinked once. "Hello, Jake," he said. He didn't give Jake a chance not to answer. "Where's Coates?"

"Dead." So he did want to know.

"Is that positive?"

"Affirmative."

"Can't win 'em all," Klein said.

"Guess not."

"Better him than you, huh?"

"You got that right, motherfucker."

239

Klein glared at him. This was the after-the-game in-the-shower debrief. The fleet halfback hadn't scored a touchdown; hadn't even given him the ball. But, it seemed, he'd gained on the reverse. He was here.

"What happened to the plant, Klein?"

"What happened to Coates, Major?"

"Last I saw of him was on his way to the plant."

"Dead or alive?"

"Couldn't tell. The plant, what happened?"

"We took it out very effectively, Major." Klein grinned. "And at the same time we got the chinks and the reds. I mean, we know what they're doing." He paused again. "We won, Major; we went three for three. Yeah. I hear your friend's in Temian. Is that where you were, Major?" Klein waved a hand. "Doesn't matter. They'll debrief in Washington. I don't give a shit what you know or don't know."

"Maybe, maybe not," Jake said. "In any case, they'll have to wait because I'm stopping off in Paris for a few days."

"Delivering messages? Changing sides? Turning? For what?"

"I can't do any of those things because I was never in the game anyway, just a decoy."

"Right, Deek." Klein turned to the window.

Silent as a shadow, and as smoothly moving, Jake was around the desk and in front of Klein; he felt the nails of his fingers digging into his palms, his hand curling into the hardest fist he'd ever made. "We've had football, and baseball, now here's a bit of the 'sweet science,' Klein." The cross struck Klein with a dull sound, lifted him out of his chair, which crashed to the floor, and sent Klein himself hurtling into the wall behind him. Klein was out.

Jake left the office, picked up his ticket, and strolled back to the motor pool to begin the drive to the airport, this time in bright, broad daylight.

E P I L O G U E

PANDEMI PRESIDENT OUSTED

RADIO BAGUI ANNOUNCES
OVERTHROW OF FASSEKE
PRESIDENT IN TEMIAN

By InterContinental

LONDON, Thursday, Feb. 24, 1966—The army said it has taken over in Pandemi and dismissed President Chuma Fasseke, who is reported to be in Temian, according to a Bagui radio broadcast monitored this morning.

Temian and its president, Taiwo Shaguri, only five days ago survived a coup that was attempted by dissident army officers.

The broadcast in Bagui by a Lt. Ngere Mbundi declared that the police had cooperated with the Army and had sealed off both the capital and the airport. All civil liberties have been suspended, and no deaths have been reported.

Mr. Fasseke assumed power in 1960, following the sudden resignation and flight of President Abraham Franklin, whose family had governed Pandemi for over a century. The nation was founded in 1830 as a homeland for freed American slaves.

Once rubber-rich, Pandemi is now one of the poorest nations in Africa, but in recent years Pandemi embarked on trade agreements with the Soviet Union and Soviet bloc nations. Some political observers believe this trading has not taken place because it was profitable to Pandemi but because Mr. Fasseke wanted to support his commitment to the East.

SOURCES SAY CIA AIDED IN COUP
THAT DEPOSED PANDEMI'S FASSEKE

By Max Reddick

May 9, 1978—First-hand, Washington-based intelligence sources said yesterday that the Central Intelligence Agency gave advice and support to Army officers opposed to the administration of President Chuma Fasseke of Pandemi in February 1966.

President Fasseke was ousted in a coup while he was visiting in neighboring Temian.

The sources said the Agency's role in the coup d'état was not approved on the upper levels of the interagency group that watchdogs CIA clandestine activities. In 1966 that group was known as the 303 Committee, and it had previously turned thumbs down on a CIA request to undermine the Fasseke regime.

President Fasseke had triggered the request by having close ties to the Soviet Union and China, sources said. The 303 Committee has been replaced by the 40 Committee.

Frequently investigated during the 12 years following Fasseke's ouster, there has never been any public revelation of a CIA role in the overthrow until yesterday. There were, however, Soviet and Chinese claims that the CIA had indeed taken part in the coup.

There was a point before Fasseke was deposed, sources said, when the CIA station chief sought approval for the use of a squad of paramilitary specialists, members of the Agency's Special Operations Group.

Sources said these experts, wearing black greasepaint, were to attack and kill everyone in the Chinese Embassy during the coup. In the process, sources said, they were also to destroy the building.

At the highest levels, after some indecision, sources said, the operation was rejected.

Nevertheless, sources said, the station in Bagui was "encouraged" to maintain contact with the dissidents in the Pandemi Army for intelligence-gathering purposes.

CIA operatives in Africa, however, believe the Agency's part in the coup against Fasseke to have been crucial, since, sources said, Kenneth Klein, the station chief at the time, received a sudden promotion to a senior post in the Agency.

"When he lucked out," one of the sources said of Mr. Klein, "we all in the Africa Division knew it. If he'd bombed, they'd have transferred him out, and nobody would have known about the CIA being there."

As the operation began to unfold, sources said, the CIA stations in Bagui and in neighboring Ulcuma and Temian were enlarged to include as many as 15 officers, all "covered," and some on temporary assignment. There was one U.S. Army Intelligence officer in the group.

Sources said that money was not a factor for the Pandemis involved in the coup, since "it was in their best patriotic interests to throw Fasseke out."

The CIA group directed by Mr. Klein got permission to buy Soviet intelligence equipment captured by Pandemi army troops during the coup. These included a camera disguised as a cigarette lighter.

Mr. Klein and other agents in the Bagui station were said by sources to have been angered by the high-level rejection of the plan to attack the Chinese embassy, which at that time, was China's single embassy in Africa.